A KID FROM SOUTHIE

*This Book is dedicated to all the kids who feel
that they have taken a wrong turn in life,
or those who feel trapped by their circumstances,
to remind them that there is always hope and
that they have the power to change.*

—John Shea

*This novel is dedicated to all the teens out there
who make tough choices; the choices carrying them
to where they find success and happiness.
And as with all my writing, this is for
Sydney and Dylan.*

—Michael Harmon

A KID FROM SOUTHIE

John "Red" Shea and Michael Harmon

WestSide Books
Lodi, New Jersey

Published by WestSide Books
60 Industrial Road
Lodi, NJ 07644
973-458-0485
Fax: 973-458-5289

This is a work of fiction. All characters, places, and events
described are imaginary. Any resemblance to real people,
places, and events is entirely coincidental.

Library of Congress Cataloging-in-Publication Data
Shea, John, 1965-
A kid from Southie / by John Shea and Michael Harmon. — 1st ed.
    p. cm.
  ISBN 978-1-934813-53-9
[1. Boxing—Fiction. 2. Organized crime—Fiction. 3. Conduct of
life—Fiction. 4. Single-parent families—Fiction. 5. Mothers and
sons—Fiction. 6. High schools—Fiction. 7. Schools—Fiction. 8. Boston
(Mass.)—Fiction.] I. Harmon, Michael B. II. Title.
  PZ7.S53753Kid 2011
  [Fic]—dc22

                                                                    2010054022

International Standard Book Number: 978-1-934813-53-9
School ISBN: 978-1-934813-54-6
Cover design by David Lemanowicz
Interior design by David Lemanowicz

Printed in the United States of America
10 9 8 7 6 5 4 3 2 1

First Edition

A KID FROM SOUTHIE

My ears rang from the repeated sharp jabs to my head in my first ever boxing match, at the All Star Olympic Gym. It was in a part of Boston I didn't go to—the rich part.

I looked across the ring at Tony Castiac, my opponent. Round two would start in fifteen seconds, and if it was anything like round one, I'd be dead in three minutes. He was beating the crap out of me.

Conor was beside me, giving me advice. "When he throws the right jab, he always drops his left arm. Trust me, Aiden. Come in with a right hook, then follow with a left. He'll be wide open."

The ringing in my ears was almost as loud as Conor's voice, but it came through. Take the jab and swing. Then swing again. Yeah. Ignore the pain. Focus. Breathe. The only problem was that the guy's jab felt like a jackhammer driving my nose into my brain. "Yeah. I got it," I said, not believing it.

Conor smiled. "You're doing fine, Aiden."

I took a deep breath. "I'm getting my ass kicked."

He adjusted my headgear. "First-fight jitters. Don't

worry about it. Just do what I said and you'll win the match. He's tired, and that means he won't be ready for it."

With the guy three inches taller than me, I'd been doing everything Conor said not to do, and I was losing. So much for my dreams of winning my first ever ranked amateur fight. I looked around the gym, full of guys I trained with, their families and friends, and over twenty fighters from across the city here just for the tournament—a full house. My cheeks stung as much with shame as from Tony's punches.

I'd busted ass for over a month to get ready for this, and now it was slipping away, just like everything else in my life. The Boston area St. Patrick's Day Amatuer Baby Golden Gloves competition would end up just another way to prove that Aiden O'Connor wasn't cut out for much. Yeah, I was a good fighter, and I'd proven it on the street a dozen times over, but not good enough for this. Not here in this ring, with this rich kid from across town beating the shit out of me.

The bell rang for round two and Castiac came in high with two jabs, followed by a roundhouse that almost took my head off. As I ducked, I instinctively crouched inside again and went to work on his ribs, cursing myself. If I stayed up he'd clock me, and every time he connected, it felt like he had horseshoes in his gloves. And I was winded. Tired. And it pissed me off.

As I came out of my crouch and backed away from his reach, my gloves at my head, he smiled. His mouthpiece glistened. "Learn to fight, Southie scum."

If the guy was working some kind of mental strategy,

he didn't know crap about South Boston Irish guys with anger-management issues. It was one thing to beat me, but it was another thing, in an entirely different universe, to trash on what I was.

Let the pain begin.

I lowered my gloves just a bit and he came in high with his jab, his left side open.

Ignoring the fist crashing into my face, I pivoted, focusing on the left side of his chin and throwing a heavy right fueled by every ounce of rage I had in me.

I landed it dead on target. Tony reeled back and, even as the impact jolted up my arm and into my shoulder, I threw the left, connecting on his nose so hard that it made him grunt.

His eyes glazed over and he wobbled, his knees shaky as I drove in and pounded his midsection with both fists. I followed with a wicked uppercut, finding the sweet spot under his chin.

Barely aware that the cheering in the gym built to a crescendo, I wanted to hurt him—and I did. Through the razor sharp rage of being so pissed off that everything was crystal clear, fluid and almost in slow motion, I nailed him with every combination Conor had taught me.

By the time Tony's eyes rolled back and his arms left guard, I knew one thing for certain: winning didn't matter right now. Nothing mattered but shoving his words down his throat with my fists and it felt good. Tony Castiac would remember me.

In another moment, the referee dragged me off him. Then the bell rang and it was over. But I didn't want it to be;

I never wanted it to end. I wanted to hammer him until he was nothing.

I stood in the center of the ring, chest heaving as I gazed at the people cheering and shouting, the edge of the razor dulled by exhaustion but the anger still burning. I felt like telling everybody to fuck off. Two minutes ago, they were cheering for my defeat and now they cheered my victory.

I knew I shouldn't feel the way I did. I should be happy, even ecstatic. I should raise my arms and wave to the cheering and clapping people. Instead, I was full of hatred for every face in that crowd. I hated them for looking at me and my tattered gloves and secondhand gym shorts, at my done-in-the-kitchen haircut and figuring that a poor boy from Southie couldn't do much more than take a beating. They were wrong, and I hated them for that, too.

The referee grabbed my wrist and Tony's. Then, as the announcer called out the victory, the ref held up my arm. I looked at Tony, regaining some of my composure. Respect, Conor taught, was earned.

"Nice match," I told him.

"Everybody gets lucky," he said.

Conor's words were blown away in that instant. "You like eating your own shit, you rich fuck?" I said, shoving him.

The ref was between us in an instant, then Conor was dragging me away. I kept my eyes on Tony for a moment, then turned to Conor. "What an ass," I said.

He scowled. "Who, you?"

I grimaced. "I won. I beat him just like you said, and

he deserved every bit of the pounding I gave him. He called me…"

He shook his head, then nodded across the room. "Have Manny get the tape off your gloves. Stick around for the awards."

As Conor hopped from the ring to get the next fighter ready, I stared at his back, confused. *Whatever*. Tony Castiac would remember Aiden O'Connor, and if Conor had a problem with that, Too Frigging Bad.

chapter 2

With my trophy stuffed in my bag and the rest of the afternoon gone after watching the remaining fights, I caught the bus home, too tired to walk. Mom would be working her butt off at the pub with all the St. Patrick's Day beer drinkers singing Irish folk songs and ordering gallons of Ireland's substitute for water. I looked forward to a big bowl of mac and cheese, watching some TV, and thinking about the fight.

Two months ago, and after coming home with another suspension under my belt for fighting in school, Mom dragged me down to the church parish, where she sat me down with Father Lamecky to talk about how I was going straight to hell for being a delinquent. The priest told her that a good way for me to get out my "good old-fashioned Irish" aggression might be to box, and then he spent thirty minutes telling me that violence only begat more violence. To turn the other cheek was the way of righteousness. Unless you were in the ring.

My way of thinking was that Father Lamecky had never been jacked in the face by some punk gangbanger who wanted the five bucks in his pocket. My other guess was that even if he did hand over the money to avoid a fight, he'd just go to the church coffers and dig out another five. That was the way of the world. But the only thing I'd ever get for not busting knuckles was five bucks lighter with even less respect, and I couldn't afford to lose either kind of weight.

So anyway, Mom hustled me down to the gym after the Father Lamecky episode, and that's where I met Conor. A bit taller than me, around thirty-five and built like a tree stump, he knew boxing inside and out. He'd grown up on the streets of Southie just like me, and he understood how it was. So I'd gone back and started training; he ran me into the ground every time I walked in the door, and I loved it.

As I made my way up the stairs to our apartment, I wondered if my dad would be proud of my trophy. There'd been a time in the past that he would have, but I didn't like thinking about when things had been better. It was another world. Another time. He was too drunk to be anything but a drunk most of the time now, and besides that, I hadn't seen him in over a month, which was fine with me. Rich boy Tony might be able to throw a hard right, but my dad's fists were a whole lot worse.

As I climbed the stairs, I remembered the last time he'd come around. Home for a week, wasted and pissed off the whole time, he wasn't afraid to knock us around because he'd had a miserable life. His dad did it to him, his grand-father did it to his dad, and he'd be damned if anybody was going to change the way drunks did business in his family.

I hated him as much as I wished I could change the way he was.

He used anything for an excuse to blow up, and the day he left, after he'd thrown Mom across the room because she'd walked in front of the TV, he busted my ear open with a bottle for telling him to stop knocking her around. He was so drunk I couldn't believe he could move that fast, and as the blood ran in streams down my shoulder, he'd staggered out the door. Gone until the next time he came home to take money from Mom.

My ear wouldn't stop bleeding, so Mom super-glued the cut. Poor man's stitches, she'd said as she dabbed it on and squeezed the flesh together.

I think I was eleven or twelve when my dad actually lived with us full-time. He'd always been a hitter, but it wasn't that bad back then. You just had to mind your business around him and avoid him altogether if he started drinking. We'd even had medical insurance through his work at B&B Grocery Distributor, along with a car, an old beater Ford Pinto, and we'd rented a house instead of living in the projects. Then he started drinking more, then more, then it was all the time, until he finally got canned from his job. That's when things really began going downhill.

Months passed with him unemployed, but cash somehow still came in. Mom never asked where he got it, but things began to change. He drank more, hit even more, yelled a lot more, and finally the cash stopped coming home. Soon he stopped coming home, too. Mom wouldn't talk about it when I asked her where he was, what he was doing, or what was going to happen, but before he left for good, I found a .38 caliber pistol in the closet.

I might have been young, but I knew right away how he'd been paying the bills.

Mom got a job at the pub, but paying rent on minimum wages and tips was like eating a Salisbury steak and pretending it was a T-Bone; you could wish all you wanted, but hamburger meat was hamburger meat and we couldn't afford anything else. So we moved to the projects, where all the other Salisbury steak eaters lived.

St. Patrick's Day was like Christmas for the Irish in Southie, and I was surprised to find my mom home. The pub should have been packed, and every waitress on the hill should have been on duty. She wasn't, though, and that was bad news.

She sat on the couch watching TV, her feet curled up under her and a blanket draped over her lap. She looked at me, taking in the puffy beginning of a bruise under my left eye without comment. She went back to watching her show. I swallowed. "Hi, Mom."

She kept her eyes on the TV. "How was the fight?"

I smiled, digging in my backpack and bringing out my trophy, which was of a boxer in a traditional stance. Below it, at the base, was inscribed:

WINNER IN THE LIGHTWEIGHT CLASS
ANNUAL ST. PATRICK'S DAY BOXING TOURNAMENT
AMATUER BABY GOLDEN GLOVES CHAMPION
BOSTON, MASSACHUSETTS

"I won." I held it up. "I beat a guy from Olympic Gym."

She picked up a mug and sipped, and from the bitter way she scrunched her face as she swallowed, I knew it wasn't coffee. A bit of it sloshed on the table as she set it down. "Joseph fired me today," she said.

"Why?"

Her face turned hard and she took another drink. "Your father says hello."

"What happened?"

"He came in the bar this afternoon. That's what happened. Just like all the other times."

I sighed. Last time he showed up at her job, he'd slapped her, then gotten into a fight with the two guys there who had a problem with a man hitting a woman. Four hundred dollars worth of tables, chairs and glasses had been busted, and Joseph, the owner of the pub, warned her that if it happened again, he'd have to let her go. Not a mean thing, he'd said, but just plain money. He couldn't afford to replace all the stuff my dad broke, and my dad broke stuff because she was there. It came to over a thousand dollars in five months.

"Did he hit you?" I wanted to know.

"No," she said, "but he broke that huge front window, which we'll have to pay for."

"He should pay for it."

"The bill will come here." She said and took another drink, this time gulping, her words slurred. "Your father doesn't pay debts and everybody in Southie knows it."

I stuffed the trophy in my pack. "I can get a job."

She raised the mug to her lips, staring at the TV. "No. My son will go to school."

"After school, then."

She shook her head. "You will not work."

She'd said it before. A Southie kid starts working when he's in school, and pretty soon he's not going to school. Then it's spending the rest of your life sweeping floors or unpacking produce at three in the morning and drinking beer for the rest of the day to forget how miserable you are.

South Boston ate people alive, she said. I just shrugged. I didn't believe that. "What are we going to do, then? Rent is due in a week."

She furrowed her brow. "Since when was it your job to pay our bills? And since when do you have anything to say about what happens in this house?"

It's not a house. It's a shitty apartment stuck in the middle of a concrete box, and the only reason we were here was because of HIM. "I'm not Dad. I can hold a job."

Her breathing quickened and her face flushed. "You are not your father, and you will never be your father. That is why you will stay in school, Aiden O'Connor. Do you understand me? No job."

"I'm seventeen. And besides, somebody has to pay rent."

"Shut your mouth, Aiden."

"Then tell me how we're paying rent, Mom. I saw the bank slip. We have forty dollars in the account, and you know Joseph's going to keep your last check to help pay for the window."

Her face twisted. "Go to your room."

"Come on, Mom," I pleaded. "I can help, too. You don't have to do everything alone."

"GO TO YOUR ROOM!"

"Mom…"

She lurched to her feet, winding back with her mug and throwing it. I dodged as it sailed past my head. As whiskey splattered my face, I wondered why drunk people threw stuff. "Get to your goddamn room, you son of a bitch, Aiden!" she said. "NOW!"

"You drunk. You don't even know what you're saying! Will you please stop?"

She sunk back on the couch. "Shut up."

"No." I stood there, wishing she wouldn't drink when things got bad, and wishing I could be somebody else, somewhere else. The fight earlier was the T-Bone steak, I realized. This was Salisbury and I was tired of eating it.

"I love you, Mom, but I'm getting a job and there's nothing you can do about it."

Then I turned around and walked out.

chapter 3

South Boston is set up like a slice of pie. And the projects, set at the bottom of the hill like the last piece nobody wanted, sucked ass. Drug dealers, thugs, bangers, con-men, thieves and addicts preyed on the hard-working people stacked up in the concrete buildings, and I shook my head as I headed down the stairs to the exit. The projects were full of everybody you either didn't want to know or didn't give a crap about in the first place.

My dad used to talk about the people living in these projects; they barely registered as human on his radar, yet now, we were here, too. The irony made me laugh. And who knows where he stayed.

As I came out into the huge courtyard facing Columbia Road, a rat scurried by my feet, racing toward the overflowing Dumpster. I avoided the corner, where three guys stood trolling for customers, baggies of dope and pills in their pockets, ready for a quick score.

"Hey," a voice called out.

I turned and smiled when I saw who it was: Tommy McAllister, loping down the sidewalk, his shadow long on the concrete cast by the street lamp behind him. He slapped me five.

"So, how'd the fight go? Get your ass kicked?"

"I won."

"No shit?"

A tinge of what I felt in the ring flared through me. "Thanks for the vote of confidence."

"Hey, man, I would have been there, but my mom flipped out again. Had to take care of Katrina."

Katrina was Tommy's six-year-old sister, and when his mom ran out of pills, things got bad. Tommy's dad, a Gunnery Sergeant in the Marines, was killed in the Middle East two years ago, and his mom went off the deep end after the funeral. Now she was hooked on prescription meds, and like clockwork, she ran out two weeks early every month. I glanced at the three guys on the corner. One of them stared at Tommy. "That your guy?"

He nodded. "Yep."

"You should get her into rehab, Tommy."

He shook his head. "Oh, really?"

"You're going to get busted buying her crap for her."

He laughed. "Nobody can catch Tommy McAllister, man. You know that. And besides, you haven't seen her go crazy. She tried to push Kat out the window last time. Three stories. Man, that would've been ugly."

"Still...buying scripts for your mom is—"

"Yeah, and if my mom goes to rehab, guess what? Kat goes to foster care, and I'd have to go kidnap her and live under a tree somewhere."

"Where's Kat now?"

"I left her with Mrs. Malone."

I nodded. Mrs. Malone was an eighty-year-old widow on the same floor as Tommy, and she watched Kat sometimes.

"I've got to get a job," I told him.

He cocked an eye at me. "Work?"

I nodded.

"Jesus, man. You start working, pretty soon you forget how to have fun."

I looked around. "This is fun? Guess I missed that part."

He stepped back, narrowing his eyes. "Whoa. You got it bad. What happened?"

"Mom lost her job."

"Your dad come in the pub again?"

"Yeah."

"What a prick."

I stuck my hands in my pockets, ignoring him. "I was thinking of Bell's Market. Maybe Lenny would hire me part time after school stocking shelves or something."

"I can get you a job."

I laughed. "I don't want your kind of job."

"Naw, come on. Legitimate. I know a guy."

If I knew one thing about my best friend, it was that he couldn't tell the difference between his property and stuff that belonged to other people. I think I was the only one he'd never stolen something from. My mom couldn't stand him, but I'd known him since third grade and he was the kind of guy who had your back. He loved Kat more than anything else, too.

"No," I told him.

He shrugged. "Your loss." Then he grinned. "You seen Angelique lately?"

I looked away. "In the halls is all. Been training a lot."

"Bullshit. You're just a pussy when it comes to women."

"Whatever."

He smirked. "Probably good that your balls haven't dropped yet, anyway. Especially when it comes to a girl like her."

"A girl like her? Like what?"

"You know what I mean."

I faced him. "No, I don't. Tell me."

"Man, this is Southie. Irish boys DO NOT, and I repeat, DO NOT, date black chicks."

"She's not black."

"Half counts, and besides, the other half is Cuban, which is like, almost black."

"Shut up, Tommy."

He shrugged, then knocked me on the shoulder. "So now, all of a sudden, you're Mr. Non-Racist of the world? I've heard you bang out some jokes before."

I had nothing to say to that because he was right. But a joke was a joke, not a person, and I didn't appreciate his mouth.

Of course he went on, because Tommy couldn't *not* go on.

"Come on, Aiden. She's a knockout, sure, but you'd get crap from all sides about her, Blacks, whites, browns. They'd all be on your ass, and that's not even taking your mom into consideration. She'd crap her pants before she'd strangle you with her rosary beads."

"Yeah." My mom would freak if she knew I was dating somebody who wasn't Irish Catholic. But I wasn't dating Angel, so it didn't matter. I just looked at her from a distance and ached.

The chances of a girl like her wanting a skinny Irish kid with blue eyes was slim to none. She could have anybody she wanted, and it totally wouldn't be me.

He looked at the guy on the corner again. "Exactly, yeah, and if you're smart, you'll listen to me. Find a nice Irish girl you can bring home to dinner, then I'll show you how to actually get her home to dinner. Then..." He knocked me again, "I'll school ya on how to make her the dessert of the evening."

I nodded to the guy on the corner, tired of listening to what I knew was the truth about where I lived, and even more tired of the black shadow in my head that made me want to jam my fist in my best friend's mouth.

"You'd better get your stuff. Looks like he's getting nervous," I told him.

"Sure. See you tomorrow?"

"Yeah." I said, and watched as Tommy walked toward his dealer to buy painkillers for his mother.

With the night settling into itself and the glow from the city proper leading me, I walked to nowhere for an hour or so, thinking about Angel and Tommy and what he'd said. The melting pot of the United States might exist somewhere, but it didn't exist here. Southie was like a cafeteria plate divided to keep your corn from spilling into your potatoes and your potatoes from encroaching on your peaches. Everybody stayed in their own section for protection and I'd never questioned it until now. Until her.

Angel, for whatever she was, didn't have a section to belong to, and I'd seen her get hassled for it by other girls who called her a mixed-breed hoe or a mutt because she was half black and half Latino. She belonged nowhere and it was a big reason I liked her. That and her awesome tits.

But unlike Angel, I did belong somewhere. I was so Irish, you might as well tattoo Ireland's flag on my forehead. And being Irish came with expectations around here. Southie started Irish, it still considered itself Irish, and every Irish mother I knew expected their kids to grow up and marry Irish Catholic, end of story. People who left Southie were instant outsiders, and people who moved into Southie just didn't belong—and they never would.

Angelique. Even her name was different. I couldn't really say I liked her personality because I'd never said a word to her. But I really thought that sometimes you could look at somebody and know them. Know how they were.

I shook my head, spitting on the sidewalk. Tommy was right. Every time I got around a girl, all the words in my head jumbled up and came out stupid. So when Tommy and Jonny Banks and all the other guys stood around talking to girls, I usually just stood there, nodding like an idiot.

By ten o'clock, the streets were still busy with St. Patrick's Day partiers, and I skirted past the bars like a shadow, avoiding the drunks out smoking on the sidewalk and staggering around, or fighting or puking in the alleys.

The cops were out in force, too, and a few rolled by as I walked, slowing down to check me out.

As I walked up the hill, I passed Joseph's pub and stopped to check out my dad's handiwork. The plate window had a sheet of plywood nailed over the opening, and glass pieces swept to the gutter glinted under the street light. I shook my head, damning him once again. Sometimes I wished he'd just die; his leathery liver finally rebelling and making him pay at last.

Fifteen minutes later I reached the gym, stopping on the sidewalk and looking at the front doors. Flashes of the fight swept through me and a shiver rippled down my spine as I remembered the power I'd felt, the control I'd had.

"You forget something?"

I turned and saw Conor walking toward me from his car up the street. I shook my head. "No. Did you?"

He smiled. "I was going to the car when I saw you. Stayed late to put equipment away and clean up."

"On St. Patrick's Day?"

He smiled. "Not much of a drinker anymore, and to me, it's just amateur day. Nothing but slobbering drunks looking for a fight."

An air of mystery surrounded Conor. He'd been a professional boxer until he was twenty-two, the pride of Southie in the middle heavyweight class. But then he'd disappeared from Southie for years, only coming back to buy the gym from eighty-year-old Jim Connelly, who'd trained him, and who still sat on his stool every day in the gym, berating every boxer within hearing.

I shrugged. "Not much of a drinker, either."

He laughed. "What, you quit the bottle when you were twelve?"

I smirked, stuffing my hands in my pockets.

"So, why are you walking past my gym this late? Only people out are partiers or thugs."

"You're out."

He chuckled. "Trouble at home, then?"

I shook my head. "Naw, not really. Just walking." I shuffled, avoiding his eyes. "You were mad today when I won."

"No, I wasn't."

"Then what? I threw every combination just like you said. I boxed him fair and square."

He studied me. "Sure did."

"Then what did I do wrong?"

His glassy eyes held mine. "Tell me why you won."

"Because I did what you told me."

He shook his head. "Not the reason. C'mon. Tell me."

I didn't like cat-and-mouse games and Conor was always full of them. He didn't talk much, but when he did, half the time it was in the form of a question; the other half it was to teach a lesson. I just wanted to box, not learn how to be a philosopher.

"I don't know," I said. "Because I got pissed."

"You liked hurting him, didn't you?" Conor said.

"Yeah. So what? That's why I box."

"No, Aiden, that's why you shouldn't box."

"He called me Southie scum."

"I know. I heard him."

I furrowed my brow. "So I'm not supposed to get

26

pissed? I'm not supposed to pound him for it? You'd do the same."

He shook his head. "I don't allow other people to control me."

"He didn't control me. I controlled him."

His face hardened. "No, Aiden. You didn't. You fought well. You didn't brawl, didn't lose your skill along with your temper. But I don't train fighters to hurt people; I train fighters to use their heads. To be smart. To succeed."

"What are you saying?"

"If I ever see you hit another person to hurt them in my gym, you can go back to street fighting."

"Then I don't need your gym."

He nodded. "Your choice."

I sighed, frustrated. "Jesus, Conor. I wanted to win, so I won."

"You can lie to me all you want, kid, but don't lie to yourself. You didn't want to win. You wanted to hurt him."

I clenched my teeth. "Well, I did win."

"No, you lost."

I stared. "Explain how I didn't win when I won, then." "No."

"Oh, so I have to figure it out on my own, right? Like usual? Another life lesson from Conor the gym guy?"

He smiled. "I'd explain it to you if I thought you were too stupid to figure out the answer yourself." He turned away, then called over his shoulder. "Make your decision, Aiden, and maybe we'll see you again."

chapter 4

Certain things in South Boston were only spoken in a whisper, behind closed doors or in the back rooms of pool halls and pubs. The whispers were as elusive and slippery as the subject—how South Boston *really* worked, and how the people you knew were more than just the people you knew.

I'd heard those whispers here and there. You couldn't be Irish in Southie and not hear them. Generations had been a part of it, and I'd always had a feeling that when my dad lost his job, he'd become a part of it, too.

Mafia.

Way back, it was the Irish and the Italians, and the two had clashed and fought for control, made peace and uneasy agreements, seen them fall apart, seen blood run in gutters, and then started over again. Famous stories, legendary ones. Organized crime. The mob.

The cycle had never changed, but now, others were part of the equation. Trade out Irish for Italian for black for Cuban or for any other people vying for a slice of South

Boston pie and you had the same thing. Struggle. This place was born struggling and it would die struggling.

Two days after I told Tommy I was going to get a job, and one day after I'd gone to five different stores looking for work only to be turned away, I walked across the school courtyard. I hadn't been back to the gym because I didn't want to face Conor and the riddles I knew the answers to. I knew what he was telling me, but he was wrong. To me, it didn't matter how you won, as long as you won.

Groaning, I kicked a rock. Mom had gone through three bottles of whiskey and home was pure hell, so I spent most of my time either shut in my room or out walking around, thinking. No gym to go to, crap at home, I couldn't find a job and school sucked. Poor me, I thought, laughing.

As I stepped from the curb next to a sign designating school property as a Gun and Drug Free Safety Zone, I watched a guy in a black Escalade parked across the street open the door and get out. He looked left and right, reached into his leather coat pocket, shook out a cigarette and lit up.

As I crossed the street and headed to the opposite corner, he said, "Tommy McAllister told me he knows you."

I stopped, turning. He wore a white button-down shirt under the leather jacket, tan slacks, sunglasses, and nice shoes, and when he lifted his hand to smoke, I saw a heavy gold watch strapped to his wrist.

"Who's asking?" I said.

He smiled, taking his sunglasses off and propping them on his head. "You're Aiden O'Connor, right?"

I nodded.

"I knew your father."

I looked at him, taking a slow breath. I didn't know this guy, but I knew this guy. I knew where the car and watch and fancy clothes came from, and I didn't want any of it.

"Doesn't mean you know me," I told him.

The smile on his face diminished a bit. "You got a mouth."

"I don't know who I'm talking to."

"Name's Liam. Tommy tells me you're looking for work."

"Tommy's the one with the mouth."

With that, his face cracked and he laughed. "You're right about that."

"I got a job."

"No, you don't."

"You don't know me."

"I know you enough." He reached into his jacket, dragging out a folded slip of paper. He held it out to me. "Here. Take it."

I did, opening it up. It was a receipt for a plate glass window from American Door And Window. "What's this about?"

He nodded toward the paper. "Joseph and I have known each other since school. Good guy. Runs a nice place. Gives me a deal on beer."

"This isn't your business."

He shrugged. "Listen, kid. I know you're trying to be

tough and you got an attitude on you. But you and your mother are in trouble and word gets around."

"So you paid for the window because you care so much?"

He nodded. "Call it a favor. Like I said, I knew your dad. And your mother."

"We can pay for it."

His eyes bore into mine, intense and black. "I'm sure you could. Like I said, it's a favor."

"I don't need your favors."

He smiled. "You call your own shots, don't you?"

I shrugged. "I don't need anybody calling them for me."

He stubbed his smoke out under his heel, opening the car door. "Fair enough. But I don't like looking out for people only to have them throw it back in my face. Especially somebody two weeks away from an eviction notice, Aiden O'Connor. I told you I knew your parents."

I knew how this worked. There were no favors in Southie, and I was stuck. Whether I liked it or not, this guy had taken on the debt we owed to Joseph, and now I was under his thumb. He'd played me into a game.

"What do you want?" I asked.

He hopped in the truck, rolling down the window. "You talk to your buddy Tommy. He'll let you know." Then he nodded, rolled up the window, and drove away.

chapter 5

My knuckles throbbed and a group of little kids riding beat-up bikes and worn-out Big Wheels stopped playing to stare. I looked back at Tommy, who stood there, nursing the bloody lip I just gave him.

He scowled. "Damn, Aiden. What was that for?"

I'd seen him down the street, walked up to him, and nailed him. "You know what it's for, man. You fucked up with me, Tommy. Big time."

A moment passed as he studied me. "What? You're going to get a part-time job while your mom turns into a drunk, and that's going to pay rent, bills and food? Come on, Aiden. Get real. You need money, and you need it quick."

"He took the debt from Joseph, Tommy! You know what that means!"

"It's not like that, Aiden. He's a good guy."

"It doesn't matter what he is. Don't you see that? The guy is serious, Tommy—big time serious, and now I owe him." I shook my head. "And unless I do whatever he wants, I'll end up at O'Brien's Funeral Home in a box with his name tattooed on my forehead." I clenched my teeth. "Thanks, man."

"It's not that way."

"You're nuts, Tommy. That guy runs Southie."

"Oh, and that's bad? Bad that he protects people? Bad that he looks out for his own? Why do you think the projects is the only place the dealers sell, Aiden? You think we don't have to deal with them on the hill because they like it down here? All the store owners and old ladies don't have to put up with their shit because of him, man. Not the cops, not the politicians. Him."

"I don't care. You screwed me."

"Well, I do care, and the only reason I said anything to him in the first place was to help you. But you just want to pretend things will get better when they won't."

He looked around, sweeping his arms in an arc. "It doesn't get any lower than this, Aiden. What're you going to do when you get kicked out of here? There's no place else to go. Be real."

"Tommy—"

"Listen, Aiden. I thought he was going to just offer you some work, not the Joseph thing—none of that. I can't help what he did, but it's his way of helping."

"I owe him now."

He squinted at me. "He paid off over six hundred dollars that your mom won't have to deal with. She'll get her last check now, right?"

I sighed. "Yeah."

"He's not a bad guy."

"What do you do for him?"

"Mule."

"You run drugs for him?"

He nodded. "And other stuff. Pick up money from people. Just simple things for extra cash."

"What does he want me to do?"

He shrugged. "He said to let him know when you talk to me about it."

I shook my head, looking off in the distance. "You're a jerk, Tommy. You know that?"

"Yeah, and you clocked me."

◆

The thing about this world was that in one moment, things could be fine, and in the next, things could get way out of hand. Several of those moments had come to pass in the last few days, and I felt like I was losing control of my whole stupid life.

After I left Tommy, I got home to my mom sitting on the couch, drinking a cup of coffee. Sober. She'd made up her face and done her hair, and even though she didn't smile when I walked in, the tension in the room was less than it had been for a while.

"Hi, Mom." I said.

"Did you go to the gym?"

I shook my head. "I was with Tommy."

She frowned. "That boy."

"He's good, Mom."

"He's a thief."

"We've been friends since forever."

She grunted. "I don't like him."

I studied her. "You went out today?"

She set the mug on the coffee table and curled into a ball, draping the blanket over her legs. "I went to four pubs looking, but nobody was hiring." She put her hand to her cheek, studying the blanket. "The Black Rose had a sign out front looking for a server, but when I talked to Donny about it, he said he'd already filled it."

"He's the manager?"

"Owner. We went to school together—before he was sent to reform school."

I took a breath. "We going to be okay?"

She sighed. "They're turning the phone off tomorrow."

"I thought we had enough to pay for that."

She smiled. "Some things are more important."

I furrowed my brow. "Like what?"

She nodded to my room. "I went through your book bag. You needed new supplies."

I looked at her. "Mom."

She cleared her throat. "First of all, I'm sorry I've been having too much to drink lately. I know you don't like it— and neither do I." She stopped, studying me. "Second, you are much more important than a phone. And please, Aiden, stay in school."

I swallowed, thinking about the mess I was in. "Yeah, I will."

"Promise?"

"Yes." I went over to her and slumped on the couch beside her, leaning against her curled-up legs. "Thanks for all the stuff."

She ran her fingers through my hair, like when I was

little. "It's a tough time right now, but we'll make it through."

"You'll find a job, Mom. I know you will," I said.

"I don't know, Aiden. The way Donny looked at me...I don't think he really had filled that position. I think word is finally out about your father. It means I'm too risky to hire."

I sighed. *Dad.* He was a foul-tempered ass, and there wasn't a person in Southie who didn't know it. "We'll make it, just like you said."

She didn't need to say anything more. That look in her eyes almost killed me, and I hated myself for feeling the way I had toward her the last couple of days.

"I know, but rent is due next week. Something has to turn up."

"You'll find a job. You will." I said, not wanting to tell her about the check she'd be getting. It would open up a whole nest of questions I didn't want to deal with.

She took a breath, stood, and walked over to her purse. "We need milk. I'm fixing Hamburger Helper for dinner. Go to the grocery for me."

I took two dollars from her. "Mom, I could get—"

She shook her head. "I'll find a job, honey. You just go get the milk. I don't want to talk about it anymore."

With two bucks in my pocket and a half-mile walk in front of me, I hustled down the stairs and decided to run. Conor had turned me on to it when I began training, and there was something about it; something freeing that came over me when things moved faster.

When I hit the street, I usually headed down toward

The Point, where I could jog along the ocean, the sea gulls squawking in the background as I breathed in the salt air.

As I jogged I realized I loved it because everything else disappeared. My mind cleared and I was able to think without everything crowding in and screwing with my head. Problems were easier to solve and there was no more anger; just the pounding of my feet on the pavement and the beating of my own heart.

As I rounded the corner, I ran up Old Harbor Street and slowed, looking ahead. Angelique was just coming from the door to a pawn shop and was walking toward me. I slowed to a walk and tried to catch my breath. God, she was beautiful.

The way she walked wasn't like a girl does. She walked like a woman. Her hips swayed just enough to almost send me to the hospital. Not a strut or awkward way about her—just a graceful, sexy movement you only saw in the movies. *Hot*, I thought. *Yeah. She was hot.*

I'd been close enough to her once to see a tiny scar above her left eyebrow, just a bit lighter than the brown sugar of her skin. I'd wondered how she got it, just like I wondered everything about her. What she liked and didn't like, what kind of food she ate, the music she listened to—everything.

Sometimes, before I fell asleep at night, I fantasized about taking her out to dinner. She'd be dressed to the nines and I'd pick her up in my new car, a Mustang GT. Low rider wheels, the color of jet, and shining like a black diamond under the moon. I'd take her for Italian. She'd like Italian. We'd drink wine, and later, we'd make love.

I shook my head, coming back to reality, realizing I probably watched too many movies. I knew I was wishing for way too much. I mean, here I was, sweating in an old T-shirt, worn sneakers, and tattered Levi's. But she had on a tight skirt, nice purple blouse, with her hair pulled back in a ponytail. As she approached, her nail-polish glinted under the street light. I held my breath, then said, "Hi."

Those dark eyes riveted on me as she walked and I realized I'd startled her. She didn't stop, but said "Hi" in return.

Panic clutched me as she swept by. I had to keep talking or lose the chance.

"You were just in the pawn shop." I said. She stopped, looking sideways at me, studying my face. I saw just a little bit of fear in her eyes.

"I'm Aiden. Aiden O'Connor. You're in my science class. Third period."

She smiled. "Oh, yes. I didn't recognize you for a moment."

I laughed, trying with everything I had in me to not be a dork. Everything about this girl was different, even the way she talked. She said *moment*, not *minute* or *second*. *Moment*. Like you'd hear ladies talk while they sipped tea or something.

"Yeah, I look like a lot of other guys." With that genius remark, I died inside. *I look like a lot of other guys? Holy shit, I might as well just slit my own throat.* But I was too busy trying to pry my eyes off her neck. Her blouse was unbuttoned just enough to show a bit of heaven. God, I was hopeless.

She let out a laugh, throaty and way too sexy. A second passed, then she nodded up the street toward the shop she'd come from. "Were you looking to buy something?"

I caught on just in time. "Oh—well, sort of. I thought I might go in and check things out. Were you buying something?"

She shook her head. "No. My father owns it. I work the counter when he needs to do inventory."

"Oh. Cool. I've seen him outside sometimes, sweeping the walk."

She laughed. "He's a neat freak."

After a long uncomfortable pause, where I could almost feel myself sinking into the concrete, I said, "Uh, sure. I bet he's very clean."

She giggled. "Yes, he is. Did you finish the science assignment for tomorrow?"

"Oh, that one. Not yet."

She eyed me, a smile curling the corners of her mouth. "That means you have no idea what I'm talking about."

I laughed. "Ya got me. I'm not too good with science," I said, leaving out the part that math, English and world history weren't far behind. "I'll get it done, though," I added.

She looked at me again. "Oh, and congratulations."

I furrowed my brow, figuring that silence was better than stupidity because I had no idea what she was congratulating me about.

She must have seen the confusion in my eyes and added, "You won a boxing match."

I perked up. "Yeah. How'd you know?"

"It was in the Southie *Tribune* yesterday. They had a

little picture of you in the sports section. I just now recognized your face from the photo."

If I could, I'd have done cartwheels down the street. I smiled. "No shi—" I stopped, reeling myself back in. *I'd been in the paper!* "Oh, yeah. It was cool. Good fight. He was a good fighter."

"They said you were 'an up and comer,' " she said and grinned.

"Yeah, well, you ain't seen nothing yet."

She laughed, then we laughed together and I was on top of the world. She looked back down the street, then at her watch. "Well, I'd better go," she said, giving me a sly look. "I have a science paper to do."

I nodded. "Yeah. Well, I guess I'll see you."

"Yeah. Tomorrow in class."

◆

I got home from the store with the milk, out of breath and delirious with thoughts of Angel. *She knew I won! She read it in the paper!* I closed the door, milk in hand, and my mom stood at the kitchen table, steaming. No, she was way past steaming. She looked at me like she wanted to rip my throat out. "What have you been doing, Aiden?"

"I went to the store. Just like you asked." I said, looking around for the sledge-hammer that was ready to fall on my head.

She clenched her teeth. "DO NOT LIE TO ME!"

I backed up a step. "I'm not, Mom. I swear. I just went to—"

"I'M NOT TALKING ABOUT THE STORE, AIDEN!" she screamed. "I'm talking about Joseph calling me not five minutes ago and telling me that the bill for the window was taken care of! That we don't owe him anything and that I can come pick up my paycheck!"

My stomach shriveled. *Fuck.* "What else did he say?"

Her voice lowered. "Nothing. And he wouldn't tell me who paid it."

"So what do I have to do with it? I didn't do anything."

She reached into her back pocket and took out a piece of paper—the receipt from the glass repair place. I'd put it in my backpack and forgotten it.

"Well, after you left, I went to put your new supplies in your book bag, and look what I found!" she said, waving the receipt angrily. Then she pointed at me. "You will not lie to your mother, Aiden! I am not stupid! You *will* tell me right now what you did to pay for this!"

"Nothing, Mom. I—"

That's when she slapped me. Hard, across the face. My cheek went numb and she went on. "Answer me," she said, her voice a growl.

"I'm not doing anything bad, Mom, I promise. Nothing bad."

A long minute passed, the muscles of her jaw working as her eyes blazed into me. Finally, she spoke.

"You will stay away from Joseph, do you understand? Do not go near him, do not set foot in his bar, and do not speak to him at all."

I nodded. "Okay. I won't."

She softened and said, "Promise me."

"I promise."

Her neck loosened, the tendons relaxing, and she looked down. "I don't want this, honey. I know where these things lead, and it's not for you, okay? My son will not become that."

"Become what? Like Dad?"

"Do not speak of him in this home," she said, then went to the sink and soaked a cloth. She wrung it out, folded it, then came back to me and held it to my cheek.

"You will go to school, Aiden. You'll study, go to college, and then you will move far away from this place. Do you understand me, Aiden? This place has ruined too much of our family already. I will not allow it to happen to you."

I swallowed. *No, I didn't understand*. I wouldn't ever understand. Southie was me, and I was Southie, and it wasn't all bad. People worked hard, played hard, and took care of family, and just because my father didn't fit into any of those categories, it didn't matter. I wasn't him and never would be.

I'd stay here, I decided. But the only difference was that I'd have that Mustang GT shining in the moonlight. I'd have one of those big condos overlooking the ocean, and I'd have Angel. And I'd get it all with gloves on my fists or without them. Either way, I wasn't going to eat Salisbury steak for the rest of my life.

chapter 6

School the next day rolled around with Tommy carrying a plastic garbage bag. He nodded when he saw me. "Hey, man. Missed you this morning. Sorry."

We usually walked to school together, but he hadn't been at our meeting spot. "Figured you were pissed because I hit you," I told him.

He smiled. "Naw. I know I deserved it."

I looked at the bag. "What's that?"

He smiled. "A present."

"Now what?"

"Dick Hickey."

I sighed. Dick Hickey was otherwise known as Vice Principal Richard Hicks, and he had a special relationship with Tommy. At over 6'3", all bone and muscle, and with an attitude that came straight from SWAT training, Vice Principal Hicks was not a person any sane individual would ever screw with. He'd been a cop in Oakland, California, for ten years before leaving to become a teacher. So the story went, anyways, but I believed it. Besides, who knew what kind of twisted reason a guy like that could have for making that kind of change.

After fifteen years, he still wore a tight crew cut, walked around like he was in the middle of a battle zone, and not a day passed when he wasn't wearing a pressed navy blue button-down shirt with the school insignia on the pocket. It was like his uniform, just like a cop.

Even when the guy talked, he didn't just talk. He commanded. I'd never heard him ask a question like, "Hey, what are you doing?" or anything else so passive. If you screwed up and he got you in his sights, you got a thick finger pointed in your face, and the words, "OFFICE. NOW!" He said nothing else, ever. Then he nailed you to the wall in the confines of his office, like he was flaying you alive. Half the school tiptoed around him like he was God with an M-16 slung over his shoulder, and rumor had it that if he smiled, his face would crack. You didn't mess with Hicks. Nobody messed with Hicks—except for Tommy McAllister.

I looked at the bag again. "Tommy, man—"

He smiled. "It'll go down in the history books. I swear."

I shook my head. "You ever think that maybe he hassles you all the time because you hassle him first?"

"Yeah."

"Why not quit, then?"

He furrowed his brow. "Why?"

I rolled my eyes. "Never mind. Just leave me out of it."

He smiled. "Wimp."

◆

Word spread all morning about something going down at lunch, and that word had Tommy McAllister plastered all over it. Paul Craig whispered it in my ear third period. *Faculty parking lot, at lunch. Be there.*

I couldn't help myself; as class let out, I headed to the parking lot with everyone else. Hicks always left school to eat lunch every day, and if you cared to notice, you'd see him without fail, heading from his office, keys jangling in his hand. He'd hop in his new truck and split to who knew where.

As I neared the fenced-in parking lot, dozens of students were hanging out, talking in small groups, waiting to see what went down.

Then I saw Tommy standing off to the side, stuffing half a sandwich in his mouth.

"Hey," I said.

He laughed, swallowing. "Thought you were too pussy for this."

"Shut up."

He shrugged.

"What did you do?"

"It's a surprise."

Just then, Vice Principal Hicks strode into view, and his neck stiffened in a heartbeat as he noticed all the kids. He scanned the perimeter as he walked, and I couldn't help but smile. He *knew* something was going on. I nudged Tommy. "He knows something's going down."

Tommy smiled. "He knows, but he doesn't know *what*. That's the beautiful thing."

I watched as Hicks reached his truck. All conversation stopped as he pushed the button on his keychain, unlocking the door. He scanned the crowd but saw nothing unusual. Then he opened his door.

I could smell it from twenty yards away. Rancid, stale, putrid and decaying, all at the same time. Hicks's face was stone as he stared into his truck, and almost a full minute passed before he moved. He reached in, pulling out a dead cat by the tail. Not just a dead cat, though. A rotting dead cat, maggots crawling in open wounds, stiff and blood covered.

I grimaced, turning to Tommy. "Tell me you didn't kill it, man."

He laughed. "No. Found it in an alley."

A sudden chill ran through me, and I wondered for a moment if he really did kill it. Tommy could be pretty cold and twisted, and sometimes I worried that his father's death had put him over the edge.

With my attention back on Hicks, he turned, holding the cat out for all to see as he scanned the crowd. His eyes settled on us. Tommy smiled, nodding his head and whispering to me.

"God, that stare could paralyze you, huh? Fucking freaks me out every time."

Tempted to step away from my doomed friend, I didn't move.

"He knows you did it."

"He knows, but he doesn't know. He can't prove anything."

"Still. He knows," I told him.

"God, that stinks. Been baking in his truck for three hours."

As dozens of students stood gaping at Mr. Hicks, he slowly walked to a green Dumpster at the end of the lot, threw the cat in, then came back, brushed off his seat, and drove off. The entire area was filled with kids who burst out laughing, talking and shaking their heads.

I smiled. "Why do you do it?"

Tommy quit smiling. "The first time he busted me."

"What happened?"

He shrugged. "He read my file, looked up at me, and told me he didn't care if I was unable to cope with losing my dad in Iraq. I would behave myself at his school, or I would be leaving. *He* was running a school and I could either man up or get out."

I nodded, thinking back to our freshman year. Tommy was having a hard time of it after his dad was killed.

"That was when you quit talking to the school counselor, huh?"

"I don't need some spy reporting to Hicks so he can throw it back in my face." Then he turned to me and smiled, slapping my shoulder. "Payback's a bitch, my brother. Come on—I need a smoke."

◆

By fifth period, Tommy proudly showed me the pink slip telling him to report to the office after school. "Interrogation," he said, adding that he might not have any fingernails the next time he saw me.

Sixth period let out, and as I grabbed my bag from my locker, Mr. Langdon called out my name. I sighed. I was failing English, and this was going to be some sort of get-your-grades-up lecture.

I turned as he met me, a beat-up leather satchel slung over his shoulder. I don't think I'd ever seen the man without at least two coffee stains on his shirt. He wore sweater vests way too often for somebody teaching in a place where wearing sweater vests could get you run out of town, and his loafers were Sixties' era relics. In fact, *he* was a Sixties' era relic.

Mr. Langdon stuffed his hands in his pockets and said, "Hello, Aiden."

"Hi."

He rocked back and forth on his feet, obviously uncomfortable. For a man who could talk eloquently about English literature for an hour straight, any other time he was like a social leper. Having a conversation with the guy was next to impossible.

"So, I saw you in the paper," he said.

I blinked, totally caught off guard. "Oh, yeah?"

"Yes. You won a boxing bout."

I smiled. "Yeah, I did."

He nodded. "It was on the front page of the sports section, in fact."

I smiled. "Cool. I didn't see it."

"You seem to be quite a fighter."

I shrugged, thinking about Conor and the gym, and how I'd avoided it lately. "Something to do."

He smiled. "The essay on *Great Expectations* is due next week."

I groaned. I'd read through the first three chapters, and as far as I was concerned, Charles Dickens could go hump a knothole because the guy obviously hadn't ever been to South Boston.

"I would guess you're enraptured with the text," the teacher said.

"If that means it sucks, yeah."

He laughed, nodding. "I presumed as much." Then he took a novel from his satchel. "And I assume, based on your previous assignments, that you won't be handing in the report."

I said nothing, wondering why I was ashamed. That book was stupid.

He went on. "Have you ever heard of John Lawrence Sullivan?"

I looked at the book and shook my head. "No."

He nodded again, handing it to me. "He was one of the greatest—and first—boxing champions of the world. He was also Boston Irish."

I took the book, which was titled JOHN L. SULLIVAN AND HIS AMERICA. "Cool," I said.

He studied my face. "You are failing my course."

"I know."

Mr. Langdon waited, a long moment passing. "I have a proposition for you."

"Oh, yeah?"

He pointed to the book. "Try reading this. Write an essay on it, and we'll forget about *Great Expectations*."

I suddenly found a new interest in the book I was holding. "For real?"

"Yes."

"I thought the school made you teach the reading list, or whatever they give you." The only reason I knew that was because everything we read was stupid or boring, and Mr. Langdon answered all our complaints by offering us the district phone number.

He rocked back and forth on his heels. "Ah, yes. The reading list. Dickens, though a fantastic writer, was a bit...dry. You hand in an essay and I'll deal with the rest. Agreed?"

I smiled. "Will I pass if I do it?"

He narrowed his eyes and they twinkled between the slits. "I'm not supposed to tell you this, Aiden, as Western Civilization might crumble, but school isn't only about grades. It's supposed to be about learning."

I looked at the book. "So I'm going to learn how to fight better by reading this?"

He chuckled. "No. You're going to learn that there are books out there that actually interest you."

"So will I pass if I write the paper?"

"No, but if you hand in one or two more assignments, you'll have a D and you'll pass."

I looked at the book. "Deal, then. And I'll try."

"Hey, Jim, come here." Conor stood at the entrance to his gym, calling back to someone inside. I sat outside, my back against the brick building, three chapters into the book Mr. Langdon gave me.

I'd thought about going in and biting the bullet with Conor, but I couldn't. Besides that, this guy Sullivan was awesome. In the late eighteen hundreds, he'd fought bare-knuckle style. No gloves, no weight classes, no nothing. Just get in the ring and start pounding. Amazing. He fought anybody, and more times than not, he won.

Jim Connelly, his weathered and leathery face in a constant scowl, joined Conor at the open door as I looked up. He frowned, swatting Conor on the shoulder as he stared at me.

"Am I seeing what I think I'm seeing? I didn't think kids today knew how to read."

I closed the book. "Hey, guys."

Conor laughed. "Nice to see you, Aiden."

Jim grinned, pointing at the book. "There's gotta' be

naked girl pictures in it." He looked at me. "You like nekkid ladies, kid?"

I stood, my cheeks burning. "I have a book report due next week."

Conor motioned to the book. "John L. Sullivan, huh?"

"Yeah. You know about him? He fought bare knuckle."

Jim and Conor looked at each other, then burst out laughing, Conor's easy and light, Jim's's like a chainsaw. Conor raised his arms, spinning in a slow circle as he gestured to the sky. "What boxer in Boston hasn't heard of John L. Sullivan? He was only the toughest son of a bitch to ever step into the ring, that's who he was."

I shrugged. "Well, I never heard of him till now."

Jim, his voice gravelly and low, smiled. "That's because you're a punk with no education." He shook his head and turned, shuffling his old body toward the door as he mumbled about the way things used to be. Jim had been around the block about a thousand times, and he was a permanent fixture in Conor's gym. Practically born with boxing gloves on, he'd spent more time in his seventy-odd years punching a bag than anything else. He'd started the gym fifty years ago, eventually selling it to Conor, who owned it for almost ten years. And now Jim sat on a stool and cussed out boxers all day, telling them they didn't know what the hell they were doing.

He'd taught Conor to box way back when, and was his trainer when Conor tried to go pro. It hadn't worked out, and the story went that Conor, at twenty years old, quit boxing and left Southie, coming back to Boston only to buy the gym years later. Now, at thirty-six, he was in the best shape of his life, but he wouldn't fight—only trained. He wouldn't even spar with me, and when I asked him about it, he shut his mouth and walked away. Nobody ever talked about the years he'd been gone or why he wouldn't fight.

Conor took a swig of water from the bottle in his hand, then called to Jim. "I'll be inside in a minute."

Then he turned to me and cleared his throat. "I'm glad you came back."

I looked down the street. "Yeah."

"You put your trophy up? Show your ma?"

I swallowed. "Yeah."

He smiled. "Good. We'll mark it as the day you learned how to live your life."

I frowned. "How's that?"

He chuckled. "Boxing ain't about fighting, Aiden, it's about using your head. So is life. You fight life, you lose. You box life, you win."

"Yeah, sure. So, what am I working today? Heavy bag?" I said as we entered the shadowy interior of the gym. It smelled like sweat and hard work, and every time I walked inside the place, I relaxed.

He pointed off toward his office. "You'll sit in my office today and read your book. Then you'll come back tomorrow with your report and I'll read it while you work the heavy bag."

I smiled. "Deal," I said, then walked to his office and sat down, cracking the book open again. John L. Sullivan was awesome.

chapter **8**

"Take this twenty down to the liquor mart. I talked to Sam before they stopped the phone service and he'll sell it to you."

I looked at the cash in her hand. "We have rent, Mom. Shouldn't we—"

"Do as I say. Now go."

I looked at her sitting there on the couch and wondered if I'd ever remember her doing anything else besides being curled up there, that damn blanket spread over her knees as she stared at the television. The coffee mug on the table was empty and by the tone of her voice, I knew she wasn't in the mood to argue; I didn't feel like having another one thrown at my head, so I dropped the subject of the rent.

"I handed in a book report yesterday. I'm getting my grade up," I said.

She tore her eyes away from the screen, those filmy orbs landing on me; unfocused and red-rimmed. She'd been drinking all day—wasted. Completely fried! She wouldn't remember a thing tomorrow.

Still focused on her booze, she slurred, "Good boy. Now go. Sam is waiting." She turned back to the screen and fumbled with the remote, turning up the volume to drown out any argument.

Bitterness welled in me. So much for her apology the other day. So much for her little speech about how we'd make it. To her, the only answer when you'd given up was in the bottom of a whiskey bottle, and I wanted to hurt her for sitting there and proving herself right about how Southie ruined people. My dad found his answers with booze, and now she was, too.

I looked around the dingy apartment with its cheap tables, Goodwill couches and dollar-store decorations. Like a vision, Angel flashed through my mind. I'd seen her in class every day since we'd talked, and today, I'd stopped her in the hall and said hello. She'd smiled at me when I did. But three guys at a locker down the hall hadn't; they'd stared at us the entire time we'd talked.

Then I looked back at my mom. *Angel isn't good enough for this?* I thought, disgusted at those guys and my mom. Fuck them. Fuck my mom. I told her, "I fell in love with a half-black Baptist girl named Angel. We're going to get married and you'll have little black grandchildren. Hope that makes you happy."

She didn't turn her head but I knew she heard me, and I knew some part of her alcohol-addled mind connected that I was picking a fight for the sake of just plain hurting her. I waited another second, suddenly *aching* for that mug to fly at me, and aching even more for it to hit me. I wanted to feel that pain, sharp and cutting and real, and I wanted her mouth to twist into an ugly sneer, the spittle gathering at the sides of her lips as the poison gushed out.

None of that happened, though. And I realized that even though we were only ten feet away from each other, we were millions of miles apart. She *did* want this. She wanted to say she'd tried at this life, but that things bigger than she was, things like my father and the projects and Southie, wouldn't let her make it or survive. It was just too hard, and if it wasn't already too hard, she'd be damned sure to make it that way. She'd find an excuse, but I wasn't going to buy it.

My mom wanted to sit on the couch with her miserable life reflected back on her through the screen of that crappy TV, proving there was nothing she could do. I hated her for it; in fact right now, I hated everybody.

So I left—because if I didn't, the urge to strike my mother, to slap her face so hard that her blood would mix with her spit, would overcome me. I guess I was my father after all, and I didn't even need a drink to act that way.

I hit the stairs and felt relief as I did. Every bone in my body screamed for escape, but I couldn't do it—that was the funny part. Because the only real way to escape myself was to pull a Tubbs Mahoney. I'd watched them that day, as they lifted his bent, twisted body onto the gurney, after he'd jumped off the roof of this place. He'd made his escape, all right.

"A Tubbs Mahoney." That's what Tommy called suicide now.

Every once in awhile, somebody at school would kill themselves, and Tommy would say they pulled a Tubbs. "Yep, pulled a Tubbs Mahoney." He'd say it with a grin and all the guys would laugh.

I'd always liked Tubbs, even though everybody gave him shit for being fat. But he was gone now, and some things sucked so much that you had to make it funny or you'd fall apart.

Tommy told me once that he envied Tubbs because somebody around here had found the balls to actually leave. And he was serious, too.

When I hit the doors, I stopped. To the left and up the hill was Sam and the Liquor Mart. To the right was Tommy's apartment.

I turned right.

chapter 9

Liam. *Lee-am*, Tommy pronounced it. Whatever.

I stood in front of the bar where my mom used to work, staring at the new window. It figured I'd end up back here. The older I got, the more I realized everything in this life went in a circle. That was the part you couldn't escape. Because everything you knew was tied to something else you knew, and I should have expected it. I'd given my mother my word that I'd stay away from this place, but here I was—for her.

I could see Joseph at the bar as I looked in. I put my hand on the door and paused, taking a breath, then went in. He looked up from the bar, blinked, hesitated a moment, then cocked his head toward a door to the right of the kitchen entrance. I had an urge to apologize for my father's mess, but I swallowed it. Let him apologize for his own mistakes—but part of his problem was that he never did.

I stared at the door. "Should I knock?" I asked.

Joseph said nothing; just picked up a cloth and wiped a glass as he stared at me, the look on his face not the welcoming smile he'd always given me before. This was different—like he didn't know me, didn't want to know why I was here. Then I understood. *I was here on business*. I paused, took a deep breath and opened the door.

Three guys were inside, including Liam. One fat dude lounged on a couch, his hands folded on his big belly as he watched a silent TV hanging on the far wall. The other guy sat at a table with Liam, who was looking through a ledger. On the wall behind them hung a dartboard with Osama Bin Laden's picture tacked to it. When I stepped into the room, all three looked up. The man on the couch sat up, his hand going quickly behind his back.

I clenched my teeth, trying to remain oblivious to the guy on the couch with the pistol tucked in his belt.

"Tommy told me to come," I said.

The guy with the belly, his old-school Boston accent heavier than mine, growled. "They teach you fuckin' kids to knock anymore? Jesus."

I forced myself to not look at the guy, staring at Liam, whose face was a slab of granite.

"I'm talking to you, kid," said the guy with the gun.

I kept my eyes on Liam. "I need to pay you back for the window, and I need to pay our rent for next month."

Liam took a moment, his eyes flickering to the big man, who leaned back, his eyes drilling into me. He closed the ledger, then nodded to an empty chair at the table. "Sit down."

I did.

Then I listened.

chapter **10**

Angel and I spent lunch together the next day at school, walking down to the Burger King on Broadway. I spent nine bucks from the twenty I didn't spend on my mom's whiskey the night before, and I did it without a shred of guilt. Besides, when I'd gotten home after talking to Liam, she'd been passed out on the couch.

I carried our tray to the table, passed Angel a napkin, and we talked over burgers and fries and milkshakes. I, Aiden O'Connor, actually talked to a girl, and not just one-word answers, either. Really talked, like I was intelligent or something.

She'd been born in Cuba, and her parents had moved to Florida when she was a year old. They came to Southie twelve years later, when her father was offered a good deal on the pawn shop. He'd been a boat engine mechanic in Florida before buying the shop, she said, and that was why he was a neat freak. Too many years of grease on his hands, she'd giggled.

She told me she liked Southie, but there was a hint of

something else in her eyes when she said it. And even though I wanted to ask her about it, I didn't—I had a feeling I already knew—she was in-between.

I'd watched her enough to be sure. I'd noticed that she rarely hung out with other girls, and I'd never seen her with a guy, even though they hung on her. As she told me about her life, I saw there was a lot more to it than just not belonging.

She worked at the pawn shop almost every day after school and that took up most of her time. I'd asked her if she made good money there and she shook her head. She told me she'd made up the part about working only when her dad did inventory. The truth was that after her father had a heart attack the year before, he couldn't work a whole day anymore. They couldn't afford to hire somebody, so Angel filled in for him.

"Family is family," she'd said, and that's when the shadow in her eyes lifted. She worked for free and somehow that meant a lot to me, because I was the opposite— every thought I had revolved around how to get money—something she didn't even care about.

That shadow came back when Angel told me that her mother had died three years ago. But as she talked about her…telling me that she'd been a singer who loved dogs, ice cream, and going to museums in Florida, the shadow lifted again. We laughed about her being dragged to what she expected to be boring, stuffy places and instead having the time of her life with her mother.

As we finished up our lunch, Angel asked me about

boxing and why I liked it, and she wanted to know if it felt good to punch somebody. I laughed and she did, too, when I told her that it did. She said there were a few people she'd like to punch. I told her I'd do it for her if she wanted me to, and then we laughed some more.

I spent that half hour in another world, one I never wanted to see end.

I knew we weren't dating—not even close, really. But after we parted and went to class, I was feeling giddy. I'd actually talked to her! I'd forgotten about what I was and what she was, and all the reasons I'd never been able to know her. And it had been…easy. Angelique Vives might not fit in Southie too well, but she sure fit me.

◆

It didn't take long. Three hours, to be specific. Out of class after sixth period, I grabbed my bag and headed toward the bus stop to go to the gym when Teddy Hollister nodded my way "Hey, O'Connor."

Teddy played linebacker for the football team and he was good; in fact, he was good enough for a shot at a scholarship. He and I didn't know each other very well, but we'd come up through the same grades together. We pounded fists and I grinned. "Hey, Teddy," I said.

"How you been?" Teddy asked.

"Good. You?"

He smiled. "Good. Listen, man, I think you're a nice guy and all, but I guess I got to tell you something."

"Oh, yeah?" I said.

He nodded. "Yeah. You know Mark Thomason, right? On the line with me."

"Seen him around."

He paused, then frowned, shaking his head. "Shit, man, you know how this goes, right?"

"How *what* goes?"

"The piece of tail you're chasing. The girl."

I tightened. "What about her?"

He shook his head. "Word ain't good, man. Mark's been jonesing over her all year, and now you're in his sights." He looked away. "Some of the guys been noticing you and her. You know. Hanging out. Like lunch today."

"So?"

"So you know how it is. That's all I'm saying."

"No, I don't know. Tell me how it is."

He backed off. "Whoa, I'm not the one all tight about it. You know how some guys are about their women."

"Oh, you mean like they own them or something?"

He frowned. "Listen, don't be getting all smart-ass with me, okay? I'm doing you a favor, is all."

I smiled. "Thanks. I'll tell you what. Tell Mark if he wants to say something to me, he can say it to my face, huh?"

"Dude, you don't want half the football team after you."

"Would that be the black half or the white half?"

He laughed. "Fuck, man, probably both."

"Including you?"

He didn't answer.

I stared at him. This guy outweighed me by over eighty pounds and I couldn't help but smile. "If *you* have a problem with me, I'm right here."

He furrowed his brow. "Don't pick a fight with me, Aiden."

I shrugged. "Looks like you're the one with the problem, Teddy."

"I ain't fighting you. We go back. That's all—just thought I'd drop you some information."

I nodded. "Next time I'm looking to own a girl, I'll keep you in mind."

"Shit, man, you're going to have a dozen guys, black and white, on your ass if you cross that line. You know it."

I turned away, done with him, then turned back. "You know what, Teddy?"

"What?"

"I don't really give a shit."

chapter 11

He owes me. Don't come back without it.

Liam's words echoed in my mind as Tommy and I trudged up the hill under a glowing, white-ringed moon.

A guy named Benjamin Capo owed Liam four thousand dollars in gambling debts, and ten percent of that would go to me if I collected. Tommy would get another ten percent. Capo owned a Laundromat on O Street and lived in the apartment above it.

I looked at the street sign on the corner. "Up around here," I said. "I know this place."

Tommy sucked on a cigarette. "I've never done this before, man. What if he doesn't pay?"

I ignored him and kept walking.

"Well, what if he doesn't? Liam will be pissed," Tommy said again.

"Maybe."

"Man, I almost have enough saved up for a month's rent," he said. "I can get Mom into rehab, and we can make it while she's there if Mrs. Malone goes along with being Kat's guardian. I need this money, man. It's important."

"Isn't your mom on disability?"

He laughed. "Ain't enough. She can't work, and her dope's expensive."

I stopped in front of the darkened Laundromat, looking to the side where an alcove hid a stairway. "Up there. Come on," I told Tommy.

We walked up the narrow stairs with brick walls on either side and came to the door. I knocked once, then knocked again.

"Who's there?" said a voice inside.

I had no idea what to say, really, so I decided to keep it simple. "Liam sent us to talk to you."

A minute passed, then we heard the chain slide. The door opened a few inches and I saw Ben Capo: stringy thin hair, a matching mustache, sloping shoulders and a middle-aged paunch. He wore cut-off sweats and slippers. He smirked. "What, he sends kids now?"

"Liam has a proposal for you. Let us in," I said, using Liam's words.

He studied my face. "A deal?"

I nodded, nervous. And, I realized, I was scared. "I'm not talking in the hall, sir."

He opened the door. We went in, and his apartment, shadowed and with only a lamp by the couch on, reminded me of ours, just minus the dollar-store picture frames. A box of Fruit Loops stood on top of the refrigerator. Next to that was a bottle of syrup. Ben Capo walked across the room, then sat on the couch. He quickly slipped a watch, a nice one sitting on the side table, between the couch cushions. I looked down and noticed that the couch legs were cockeyed, like it had just been moved. He sat back. "What kind of deal?"

Tommy stood to the side and I turned my attention to Capo and nodded. "You pay Liam four thousand dollars tonight."

He smirked. "He'll get his money."

I sighed. "Sir, if you don't pay us now, we have to hurt you. And I don't want to do that."

He studied my face, maybe wondering if I had it in me. "I don't have the money. I told him that."

"Yes, you do."

He shook his head. "Listen, kid, I don't know who you think you are, but Liam and I go back—way back. I've always paid my debts to him."

I nodded to the couch. "That watch goes for what? A thousand? Two?"

He swallowed.

"You have one minute," I told him.

"What?" Capo said.

I stepped forward, smacking him across the forehead. He jolted backward.

"One minute," I said. "Get the money."

He touched his forehead. "Hey, hey, hey, no need for that. None. I'm peaceful. Things have been rough, is all."

"Please, Mr. Capo. Don't make me do this."

"I told you, I—"

"Get up," I said.

He didn't.

"GET UP!" I repeated.

He did, and I walked to the couch, shoving it away

from the wall. A section of carpet was loose at the molding so I yanked it up, exposing a small compartment in the floor boards. I opened it and reached inside, pulling out two stacks of bills. I straightened. "How much is here?"

He pleaded. "Five thousand. But listen, kid, that's not mine. I'm betting on a horse for a guy I know. It ain't mine. You can't take it."

I tossed it to Tommy, who stood wide-eyed. "Count out four thousand."

Ben Capo rubbed his forehead. "If you take that, I'm dead. You understand? Liam will understand. He will. Just go back and talk to him. Tell him I'll pay him by next week."

"I'll be out on the street by next week, sir. I need it as much as you do."

Tommy handed me back a thousand dollars.

I dropped the cash on the table, turning to Capo. "Liam wanted me to let you know that his credit is still available to you. He said you go back." I paused. "But he also wants you to know that next time, it won't just be a threat."

chapter **12**

"Okay, tell me one thing. How did you know there was money under the couch?" Tommy said.

I smiled as we walked, not a bit nervous, even with four thousand dollars stuffed in Tommy's jacket pocket.

"Remember our old house?" I asked him.

"Yeah, on 7th Street."

"Mom used to hide spending money under the couch." I shrugged. "The couch in his apartment had been moved. The carpet dents didn't match up."

He laughed. "Damn, you should be a detective."

I chuckled. "I could tell when Mom put more money under there because of the slide marks, so I used to look every time I went home. Sort of caught my eye in Capo's place."

He coughed. "You were intense in there."

"I guess."

"That was awesome." He smiled. "The look on your face was cold. Real cold."

I shrugged. "We need the money, Tommy, and guys like that don't give up anything. You have to *make* them."

He crumbled into laughter. "Dude, did you see him when you smacked his forehead? The guy looked like he got struck by lightning. Funny stuff."

"My share is four hundred. I need a hundred more for rent, plus I have to pay off the window."

"Yeah."

"Then I'm done." I looked at Tommy. "Understand that? No more. You get your mom in rehab, fix things with her, and that's it."

"Sure," he said.

I cocked an eyebrow at him.

"Okay, yeah. No more after that."

We walked farther on, and as we neared Joseph's bar, I stopped. "I need to know something."

"What?"

"Why can't my mom find a job?"

He screwed his eyes up at me. "How would I know?"

I looked off toward the pub. "You didn't hear any-thing?"

"No." He paused. "Probably your dad, though. Why?"

I shrugged. "No reason. Come on."

chapter **13**

"The match is in a week. You think you're up for it?"
Conor said.

I stopped punching the speed bag. "Yeah. Sure."

"Good. I'll get you signed up. It's a big one."

"How much?"

"Registration is eighty dollars. I can loan it to you if
you need it," he said.

I punched the bag again. "No. I can scratch it up."

He studied me for a moment, then nodded. "Okay. I'll
start the paperwork, then."

"You said there will be guys from other cities at this
one?"

He nodded. "The New England Golden Gloves brings
'em in from all over. You'll be marked as official with the
New England Amateur Boxing Association."

I smiled, excited. "You really think I can do it?"

He laughed. "Wouldn't ask if I didn't think so." He
threw me a bottle of water. "How's school?"

"I'm passing everything now. My English teacher let

me pick another boxing book for my next assignment, and it brought me up to a D."

"Good guy, huh?"

"Sort of like he's not even a teacher, you know? Not all hardcore with the rules, even though he's weird."

"Good. And how's your mom? New job, I take it?"

"Not yet. Why?"

He nodded, almost to himself. "Just figured she'd have landed something by now." He paused. "You sure you don't need that eighty dollars for sign up?"

I took a breath. "I got it. Been doing odd jobs after school."

"Oh, yeah? For who?"

I shrugged. "Just neighbors and stuff."

He smiled. "Wow. That, *and* getting your grades up? Busy guy."

I grinned. "Yeah."

He looked at me. "You could go pro someday, you know."

"Pro what?" I said.

"Boxer."

I studied his face, looking for the catch, the joke. But there wasn't any.

"I've only fought one match, Conor."

He shrugged. "Did you ever see Larry Bird play basketball for the Celtics?"

I shook my head.

He chuckled. "Was a long time ago. Anyway, the guy was the most awkward-looking human being to ever pick up a basketball, but when he did, you knew in a heartbeat he was a natural. He was meant to do it."

"You think I'm meant to box?"

"Yes. Six months of hard training, along with the right matches, and we could make a go of it. You could make a career of it, Aiden."

"You're bullshitting me. This is some kind of 'keep the kid out of trouble' talk, right?" I smiled.

He shook his head. "You could *be* a professional boxer."

I took a breath. "Okay."

He nodded. "You need to build your strength without leaving your weight class. We'll be working on that, but for that to happen, I need you here more often."

A ripple of excitement went through me. *Pro. I could go pro!* "Deal," I told him.

He eyed me. "No. The only deal is that you stop working those 'neighborhood jobs.' "

My breath caught. "It's just odds and ends until Mom finds work. We need money."

A moment passed. Then he spoke, and a shadow seemed to cross his face. "Southie is a small place, Aiden."

I thought about asking what he meant, but I knew. Word got around quickly, and I didn't want to have this conversation. This part of my life was separate from that part.

I sighed. "Mom can't find a job."

He stared at me. Not a hard look, but more…searching. "I know it."

chapter 14

I rounded the corner of the gym after school the next day and found Mark Thomason standing in front of Angel. From the frown on her face, I could tell something was going on. I came up behind him and said, "Hi, Angel."

Stress tightened her face and her eyes flicked to me.

Mark turned and I smiled. "Hey, Mark. What's up?"

He turned his big head, which was attached to his big body. "Just talking to your girlfriend."

I smiled. "Didn't know I had one."

He faced me. "I was inviting her to a little party we're having this weekend. You don't mind, right? I mean, seeing that you're not dating?" He said, his eyes twinkling.

I shrugged. "No problem at all. Thanks for checking in with me, though."

He bristled. "I wasn't checking in."

I nodded, blowing him off. Then I smiled at Angel. She was going to look over the rough draft of my next English paper, and I wasn't interested in a big black guy trying to pick a fight with a skinny white kid over a Cuban girl.

"You ready?" I asked her.

She nodded, the stress still lingering on her face.

Mark didn't let up. "I said I wasn't checking in."

"I heard you."

His face turned hard. "Don't be a punk, O'Connor."

I smiled. "I'm not going to fight you, Mark."

"Yeah, you're not, because you're a pussy." He looked at Angel. "Why you hanging around this clown? The guy is a joke."

She clenched her teeth. "Don't, Mark."

He looked at me. "You're a clown, O'Connor. You know that?"

"Sure, Mark. Whatever you say."

He shoved me. "Yeah, whatever I say."

Angel stepped between us. "Stop it, Mark. Just stop!"

He laughed. "You need a chick to protect you now?"

I shrugged. "I'm not interested in fighting."

"How about I make you interested? Huh?"

I thought about Conor, and about boxing, and how I shouldn't fight mad. But it was hard not to want to pound his face, even if chances were I'd lose.

"I don't think you can make me interested, Mark."

He shoved me again and this time I swung, nailing him hard on the side of the throat—the sweet spot. I could feel it. He reeled back, grunting, and went down to his knees, choking as he brought his hands to his neck. His face turned a deep shade of purple, and his eyes bugged out as he tried to catch his breath.

Angel stepped forward as he struggled to breathe, panic on her face. "He can't breathe, Aiden."

I looked at him, and I almost walked away. "He'll be fine," I said, but I wasn't sure. He couldn't breathe, and people were gathering around. Angel shouted for somebody to call 911 and I watched cell phones pop open. Mark was on his hands and knees, his neck strained, muscles bulging as he tried to inhale. Then he went limp, his body sprawled on the concrete.

Angel screamed.

chapter 15

"My people don't draw attention to themselves."

I looked at him. "I'm not 'your people.'"

Liam sat back in his chair, in the back of the pub. A cigar lay smoking in an ashtray on the table. George Lilly, the fat man with the pistol who never seemed to leave the couch, stopped watching the television and sat up, his hand moving toward his piece.

Liam waved him off. "No need for that, Lil'. Aiden and I are just having a conversation."

I stared. "Tell me why my mom can't get a job."

A small smile curled his lip. "What does *that* mean?"

"I mean every pub in Southie that's hiring won't touch her. Tell me why."

He sat forward, tense. "What are you saying?"

"I'm saying I'm not one of your people, and I'm done working for you. My debt is paid."

"I'm not connecting here, Aiden."

I stood. It didn't matter if he'd scared everybody away from my mom like I thought. I was finished working for this guy, and we'd make do somehow.

"I'm done with you," I said.

"Sit down," he told me.

I didn't move.

Liam's eyes flicked to Lilly. The big man stood, walked over, put his hands on my shoulders and shoved me back down into the chair.

Liam nodded. "You're not done, Aiden. You've got charges pending against you for crushing that nigger's throat, which means I've got a problem with one of my boys drawing attention to himself." He paused, letting it sink in. "You're not done at all."

"I didn't crush it, and he's not a nigger," I said, frustrated and nervous all at the same time. I might have my head on the block for it, but every time somebody said that word, I got pissed.

He shrugged and looked at Lilly, then back to me. "You go to lockup, your mom still doesn't have a job. Where does that leave her, Aiden?"

"Bastard," I said.

He smiled. "I'm not your enemy, Aiden. I'm just pointing out the practical side of your situation. Giving you advice."

I took a breath.

He folded his hands on the table. "I'll take that as an agreement."

"What about the charges?" I asked. "They said it was a felony."

"I talked to a buddy I know down at the precinct. The district attorney will be filing misdemeanor charges against you. You'll get a slap on the wrist."

A full minute passed as my thoughts reeled. There was no way out.

"And what do you get?" I asked him.

He smiled. "An agreement with you to keep doing my jobs."

chapter 16

"You could have killed him."

I sighed. First my drunk mom blasted me, then the school expelled me because I dared to touch a football god, then Liam put my head in a vise. And now Conor was sitting behind his desk, staring me down. There was no place that somebody wasn't banging on me.

"Yeah. So?" I said.

He shook his head. "Aiden…"

"What? What do you have to say about it?" I glared at him. "You want to say I was wrong? That I shouldn't have done it? That I should have walked away? I tried, Conor. You weren't there. If you commit a felony, which it was, on school grounds, you're out. End of story."

A long moment passed, and then the expression on his face changed. Softened. "Your mom still looking for a job?"

I looked at the calendar on the wall marked with up-coming bouts. "She's too busy being drunk."

He nodded. "I know how Southie works, Aiden."

"Well, I don't. And I don't really care, either."

"You know Casey Taylor? Guy comes in and works the bag every week?"

"Yeah."

"He's a detective down at the station."

I shifted in my seat. "So?"

"So he let me know your charges were reduced."

"Is that your business?"

He grunted. "Just talking."

"About what?"

He clenched his teeth. "Don't get hard-ass with me, Aiden. I know what this is about. I know what you've been doing and it's dangerous. Liam is not a man you want to know."

"You don't know shit."

His eyes went flat, level as a frozen lake. "Yes, I do."

I stood and turned toward the door. "Later."

"Sit down."

I faced him, my neck hot, blood pounding in my ears. "Fuck you, Conor. Don't tell me what to do. You have no idea what my life is or what I do, so eat shit."

"I can help you."

Tears welled in my eyes, and the rage that had been building exploded like a keg of dynamite. "For what? What do you want? Nothing is for free in this place, right? So, what is it, Conor? You want me to suck your ass? Wash your car? Sweep your fucking floor for eight bucks an hour so I can be a loser for the rest of my life?"

My chest heaved and my heart beat a million miles an hour. I stared at him, and right then, he was just like everybody else in this town.

"I don't need nothing from nobody, and I don't need this shit from you," I said.

Then I left.

chapter 17

"I'm going running."

She turned away from the television, her bleary eyes searching the room before they came to rest on me. "Go to the liquor store and get me a bottle."

"No."

She leaned her head back, staring at the ceiling, her words so slurred I could barely understand them. "Aiden, please. Just go get it."

"I'm not buying your booze."

"Do as you're told."

"No, Ma. I'm not doing it."

Staring at the ceiling, she yelled at me to get her the bottle; then, when I said no again, she stood, swaying dangerously before losing her balance at the coffee table. She crashed on top of it, arms flailing, coasters, cups and a plate with a half-eaten tuna fish sandwich scattering as she smashed down on top of it. She rolled to the floor and lay still for a moment. Then, in a stupor, she tried to get to her knees.

Sickness crawled deep into the pit of my stomach as she tried to stand. She was no different from a drunk in the gutter. From her knees she tried to stand, once again losing her balance and plopping back down. She sat there, looking around like she'd landed in a foreign place. Drool hung from her gaping mouth in a long thin line reaching the front of her nightgown. She moved in slow motion.

"Go get it!" she cried, her mouth an ugly gaping hole.

I stood there, silent.

Her eyes rolled then, and I sprang to the kitchen, slamming open the cupboard door and grabbing a bowl.

Running back into the room to the sound of retching, I clenched my teeth. On her hands and knees, and with her back arched as she spasmed, she let out guttural, muscle-pulling chokes and sobs as I bent and held the bowl under her mouth.

But I was too late. A pool of brownish green puke covered the carpet, shining under the lamplight, even with the one bulb burnt out. I set the bowl on the liquid and stepped back, waiting for her to finish. She reminded me of a stray dog in the alley, vomiting up rotten food and gagging on its own mistake.

After more guttural and spastic retching, she leaned against the coffee table and rested her head in the crook of her elbow as she wiped the vomit from her face, smearing it across her cheek.

Tears of strain ran down her face from eyes blood-shot and filmy, and I didn't want to look at her. I didn't want to see that booze-puked-and-stained nightgown, or those damning eyes that looked so much like mine. Her ratty hair tied in a bun and the filth on her sloppy, drunken face made me wish I didn't know her.

Bile rose in my throat and I turned, walking to the door. I opened it, thinking this couldn't be my mother. My mother would never be like this.

"I'm going running," I told her.

I waited. She said nothing. Tears welled in my eyes as I stared at her. Damn this, and damn God for ever putting me here.

I couldn't leave her. I shut the door, turned and walked over to her, speaking softly. "Come on, Mom." I hitched my hand under her arm and lifted her frail frame to her feet. "Come on. Over to the couch."

As I helped her, she mumbled something about her father, but then I noticed a thin stream of blood running down the back of her neck. As I lay her down, I took a closer look. She'd hit her head on the corner of the table.

I went to the kitchen, put a towel under the hot tap, wrung it out and went back to her.

She'd passed out and was lying there on the couch with her eyes half open and her mouth slack and wet. I sat next to her, wiping her face and neck, moving her head to check the cut. Not that bad. The bleeding had stopped so I lay the towel on the table, then turned her on her side so she wouldn't choke if she puked again.

The entire apartment smelled like vomit and rotten whiskey, and she'd peed on herself while she was retching. I sat there next to her, my hand on her shoulder, listening to her breathe as I looked around our dollar-store-decorated shit-hole. I wondered how close she was to dying from alcohol poisoning.

I was too worried to go out so I just sat there for awhile and thought about a lot of things. Finally, when she seemed okay, I left for my run.

chapter 18

With my feet hitting the pavement and the cool night air pulsing around me as I ran, I tried putting everything out of my mind. My mom was contagious and I couldn't let her bring me down. Everything didn't have to get worse, and memories weren't the only thing that could be good. I had a future, and Southie was part of it. Southie was in me, and I was in Southie.

But the usual freedom of running wasn't there and it made me angry. This time I was running to run away from something, not running to be free. After the first two miles I stopped, leaning against a light post and catching my breath.

He did this, I thought. If my father hadn't become a drunk, none of this would be happening, and the part of me that wasn't angry about it wondered one thing: why? *Why had he chosen this for our family?*

Looking up the street, I shook my head and spit. No. I make my own choices. He might have put us here, but I'm in charge now, and I'm not afraid of him anymore.

So I ran.

I ran with my mind on what was ahead of me, and I knew where I was going. Ten minutes later I stopped in front of a pub. The owner, a guy named Lonny, was old school with my dad, and I figured if he'd be anywhere, it'd be here. I remembered when Lonny would come over to the house for dinner sometimes, and he and my dad would sit on the porch and drink, talking about life.

I was right. When I opened the door, the first person I saw was Nick O'Connor, otherwise known as my dad. I wiped the sweat from my forehead as several heads turned at the sound of the bell above the door. My dad, slouched on a stool at the bar with a half-empty beer in front of him, didn't look up. Lonny blinked, frowned, then recognized me. He smiled. "Well, Jesus, if it isn't you, all grown up."

I nodded to him, then looked at my dad. Hunched over his beer like a haggard old lion protecting a bone, he turned to me. He looked tired, and his skin was sallow and loose. I knew he was forty-seven years old, but he could have been sixty.

He wore a Boston Red Sox hat and graying hair poked out around his ears. Dressed in jeans and a worn Windbreaker, I realized he fit into this bar much better than he fit into our lives. It didn't make me mad, though, and my anger actually disappeared. He was what he was, and I wasn't here to be pissed at him. I was here for another reason.

With his head cocked at me, he didn't say a word. Just looked. I walked down past the few stools toward him and sat down to his left. My dad looked at Lonny. "He okay in here, Lon?"

Lonny nodded. "Sure, Nick. For a few." He looked at me. "You want a Coke, Aiden?"

I shook my head. "No, thanks."

Lonny looked at me for a moment, then poured a beer from the tap, setting it in front of another patron down the line. I looked at the bottles behind the bar. My dad did, too, then took a long pull from his glass. "Something wrong?" he said.

"No."

"Your mother okay?"

"Other than you getting her fired, yeah. She's passed out drunk at home."

He shook his head, his gravelly voice slurred, but menacing. "You here to put things right? Now that you're a man? Defend your mother's honor and all that?"

"No."

He chuckled, lighting up a cigarette. "Saw you in the paper. Gonna be a boxer, huh?"

"I'd like to, yeah."

Silence. He slowly tapped the bottom of his glass on the bar. "Can't say you don't got it in you. O'Connors' are fighters."

"Sure."

He took a drag, inhaled deeply, then let it out. "You beat him good?"

"Yeah."

"Good," he said, swallowing the rest of his beer. I guessed it was the closest thing he could get to telling me he was proud. He motioned to Lonny, who poured him another. A moment passed, then he said, "I'm wondering why you're here."

"I was out running."

He snuffed his half-smoked cigarette out, shaking his head and staring at the bottles. "Just like your mother."

"How's that?"

"Fucking liars. Both of you."

I shrugged. "I was out running. And thinking."

"What? You want money? I ain't got none."

"No. I took care of the window myself," I said.

He looked at me for a moment, anger in his eyes. He looked away. "Then what do you want?"

"I want to know why."

"Why what?"

I took a breath. "I want to know why it's like this."

His face darkened.

I went on, trying to backpedal before he got pissed. "I mean, things were good, Dad. Before we moved to the projects. We had the house, a car, all that. And now it's just...." I said, not knowing where to go with it. "I just want to know why it all went so bad."

He lit another smoke, throwing the lighter on the bar. He shook his head again, then looked down to Lonny, calling out. "Hey, Lonny, my son here wants to know why his life is so frickin' hard. You got an answer for him?"

Lonny looked up from the sports section of the paper and smiled. "Sure don't, Nick. We all got it hard one way or another," he said, then went back to reading.

My dad swiveled his head toward me. He talked low, his mouth tight. "You come in here whining and sniveling to me about how shitty your life is? Is that it? You come to see your old man to blame me for all your problems? You got no idea about anything."

I swallowed and it hit me that I wasn't here to understand *why*. I was here because I wanted it back. I wanted my old dad back, not this drunk sitting here, cussing me out. I wanted both my parents back the way they used to be.

"I didn't mean it that way," I said. "I just…maybe if you quit drinking and came home, we could start over? Things could get good again, you know? Like they were."

He took a breath, then swigged half his beer, clanking it down. It sloshed, spilling on the bar. He looked at me, studying my face for a moment. There was pain in his expression, and I didn't know where it came from. He coughed and said, "You know what's good for you?" He stood up, unbuckling his belt. "You need yourself a goddamned whipping, that's what you need. You don't talk that way to me, telling me I ruined your life, you insolent little shit." He slid his belt from the loops. Lonny saw it from the end of the bar and stood up from his stool.

I got up from my seat, glancing at Lonny. "Dad— don't. I didn't mean it that way."

He twined the leather around his hand, swaying on his feet as he did so.

"Dad—"

He reared back with the belt, ready to swing. I jabbed him in the chest, pushing him back. He banged against the stool, losing his balance. I blinked and a second later, he hit the ground with a thud, stunned as he stared at me.

I shook my head. "I didn't come here for this."

He clenched his teeth. "Get out."

I looked at him. "You got out a long time ago, Dad. And you're a coward for it," I said.

Then I left.

chapter 19

Tommy strutted his way across the courtyard wearing a new gold necklace, a pair of ridiculously bright, flashy sweats and new shoes. And he had a new iPod clipped to his waist. He pulled out an ear-bud and powered it off.

"He's dead, dude," he said.

"Who?"

"Ben Capo. The guy we got Liam's money from."

"What?"

Tommy nodded. "The dough we took wasn't his, just like he said. They found him down at the water by Kelly's Landing with a plastic bag tied around his neck." He chuckled. "Hard to breathe that way, I guess."

"Jesus."

He shrugged. "I guess he was telling the truth when he said they'd kill him."

I had nothing to say. My stomach flip-flopped.

Tommy punched my shoulder. "Hey, man, we didn't do it, did we? He was a sucker."

"He's *dead*, Tommy."

"He's dead because he made himself dead. Not me."

"Maybe, but we helped him get there."

He shrugged. "Not my problem. I just do my job."

Something in me emptied out as I pictured Mr. Capo dead. What was I becoming? Was this me? A man died because I'd "done my job," and my best friend didn't seem to mind it at all.

"I thought we were done," I said.

He laughed. "Fuck that. I like money. And besides, from what I hear, you're not done either."

"We had a deal."

"*You* had a deal, Aiden." His eyes softened. "Come on. Please. I'm not going to live in the projects for the rest of my life. Plain and simple."

I faced him. "You like it, don't you?"

"What's not to like about money? Listen, Aiden, nobody screws with me now. You remember Corey Lawson from last year? The guy ragged on me every chance he got because he's an ass."

"Yeah, I remember."

He laughed. "I knocked him into a locker yesterday when we passed in the hall. Know what he did?"

"What?"

"Nothing. Just kept on walking. He knows I'm connected."

"Great, Tommy. That make you feel good?"

He grinned. "Why wouldn't it? It's all about power, Aiden. Don't you get it? Come on, man, you're not going to Juvie because of that power. We're both making money, and we could be on top of Southie if we play things right. What's wrong with that?"

"Everything."

"Liam brought me up a few days ago. I got four guys dealing under me now. I just supply, collect, and pass it along to Liam, and he's also giving me bigger stuff to do, too. Business-end stuff, like Capo." He paused, taking a cigarette out, lighting up and looking around. "There's so much stinking money in Southie. You wouldn't believe it."

"You're making a mistake, Tommy."

He shook his head. "You're fighting the wrong thing, man. You could spend your life getting the shit knocked out of you in a boxing ring, trying to make rent every month, or you could be a king in this town. We both could be kings."

"I could go pro."

"Maybe, but you ain't going to be the next Sugar Ray or Marciano, that's for sure."

"Maybe I *could* be."

He stared at me. "I made eight hundred dollars last week, plus another two for driving up north with Lilly to collect from a difficult client." He smiled. "Lilly is a madman with a baseball bat, by the way. You should have seen it."

I clenched my teeth, sick to my stomach.

He stared at me. "How much did you make last week, Aiden?"

"I'm not talking about this."

He smiled. "How much, Aiden? Tell me."

"Go away, Tommy."

He looked at me. "Don't be a fuck-up, Aiden. Liam is doing you a favor."

"Is that what Liam is feeding you? That blackmail is a favor? He's a thug."

He smirked. "Watch your mouth about him, huh? Things like that get heard by the wrong ears and you'll find he won't like it much."

"Like *your* ears, Tommy? Is that what you're saying?"

He stared at me. "I just don't want to see you get on his bad side. That's all. And by the way, Lilly doesn't like you, so don't turn your back on him."

"Lilly is a fat fuck-tard with an attitude, and besides, I don't wear a leash around my neck."

He laughed, understanding the jab. "The only leash I wear is worth eight hundred bucks a week. So stick it, Aiden. He kept you out of jail, and you're sitting here tearing him up. He *helped* you."

"I didn't need help."

"Well, you got it. And he wants to see you tonight. Eight, at the pub. You owe him."

I studied his face, wondering what had happened to my best friend in the last couple of weeks. "You get paid for telling me that, Tommy?"

He didn't smile. "I get paid for everything now, Aiden." He stopped then, and the look in his eyes changed. "And by the way. I wouldn't mention anything about Capo to anyone. We were the last ones to see the guy, and you don't want the cops beating your door down."

I looked away. "Yeah."

Tommy nodded. "Good. You just got to get your priorities straight, man. We can do this. We can make good."

I furrowed my brow, looking at his new clothes, his bling and his iPod. "So, I take it you had enough money to get your mom into rehab?"

The look in his eyes sharpened. "Some things don't work out."

I nodded. "Nice getup," I said, motioning to his clothes.

"Fuck you, Aiden."

"Priorities, right?"

He flipped me off, then walked away.

chapter 20

"I had no idea that would happen," I said. "I swear."

Angel stood with her arms crossed behind the counter of the pawn shop. I hadn't seen her in the three days since messing up Mr. Football's windpipe, and not being at school, I missed her. She looked at her fingers on the glass counter. "They said he almost died."

Heat rose to my cheeks and I swallowed. "He started it, Angel. I tried not to get into it with him."

She sighed. "I know, but…"

"But, what?" I stared at her. "Oh, I get it. You don't want to be with me because I'm a street punk? Some thug?"

"No. I just…." She exhaled. "Aiden, we're just very different people, you know? I guess I'm not used to it. To how you do things."

I grunted. "So that's it? You're breaking up with me and I didn't even know we were dating. Damn."

She looked down again. "No, I'm not. But this is becoming complicated."

"Like, how?"

She rolled her eyes. "You *know* how."

"School?"

"Yes. And my dad."

"Because I'm white?"

"My father would like me to date Cubans. He's old fashioned that way, and he also wants…good things for me. Don't you understand?"

Rage boiled in me and overflowed in an instant. "Yeah, I do. I'm poor white trash, and that's not good enough for the daughter of a dirty wetback who paddled to America on a fucking ten-dollar raft." I steamed. "Your father is a piece of crap, and if he was here right now, I'd—"

Anger flared in her eyes. "You'd what? Beat him up like you did with Mark?"

I knew I was about to do what I always did when I got mad—destroy things. I looked at her, took a breath, then another, then spoke. "No, I wouldn't hurt him, and I shouldn't have disrespected your father. I don't really think of him that way, but he has no right to judge me like that."

I licked my lips, wanting to turn this around. "I really like you, Angel, and if you don't want to see me anymore, that's fine. But if it's because of those other things, that's not right and you know it."

She swallowed and my insides melted. The last good thing in my life was slipping through my fingers and I felt powerless to stop it.

Then Tommy's words hit me like a hard right. *We can be kings.*

"I want to be with you, Angel, and if you give me the

chance, I can make you the queen of Southie. We can have everything."

She smiled, avoiding my eyes. "Aiden…"

"Do you like me, Angel?"

"Yes."

I nodded. "Then why don't we just leave it at that for now, huh?"

She hesitated. "Things are just…bad right now. School is bad, my dad isn't well, and I just don't want to see you get hurt because of me."

I stared at her. "School is bad?" I studied her. "Who's giving you shit?"

She frowned. "No, nobody is. You know how people see things is all."

I shrugged. "Fine, then. I like you, you like me, we'll let it slide for now. Deal?"

She nodded. "Deal."

I smiled, then leaned over the counter and pecked her on the cheek. "Okay, then. See ya."

chapter 21

Ross Talbott Knight looked like he thought he was going to die.

I knew him for five hundred dollars—that's how much I was getting paid to visit him. Liam controlled most of the construction cleanup in Southie, and Mr. Knight sat on the planning and zoning commission for the city of Boston. He was new to the job, and he was holding up the zoning process on a seventeen-million-dollar construction job down near The Point, on the east side of Southie. Liam didn't like his deals being held up.

White as a sheet, eyes bugging and chin quivering, he had tears in his eyes. He looked like a nice guy. I wondered if he'd ever been married. He looked to be in his fifties, maybe even had grandchildren, just a guy from the West Coast who wasn't used to this kind of business. Liam said he'd taken the job from Los Angeles—land of Hollywood starlets, beaches, glamour and lots of money. Liam chuckled when he told me about him. "Give him a nice Southie welcome, Aiden," he'd said.

I looked at the guy now. He reminded me of my fourth-grade teacher, Mr. Prichard, one of the best I'd ever had.

I reasoned with him. "Mr. Knight, please do as I say. Do you understand?"

He nodded. He couldn't talk because I'd carefully placed six razor blades on his tongue. Personal protection insurance, Liam called it. You've got to come on hard and fast, not only to get what you want, but to make sure you walk away alive.

"You know that job down near The Point?"

He didn't move for a moment, his eyes searching mine. Drool, tinged red, gathered at the corner of his lips. I realized he'd thought I was going to rob him, and I could see on his face that the truth was beginning to dawn on him.

"You know it, right?"

He nodded.

"The man I work for told me to let you know that if there are any more problems with the zoning, it won't be a good thing for you. Do you understand what that means?"

He nodded. His left eye twitched. The man was terrified, and I'd never seen anybody so afraid.

I studied him, seeing the fear and dread and revulsion coursing through him as he wondered what the next few minutes held. The guy was just doing his job, but so was I. *Just doing my job. Yeah. Just like with Ben Capo.*

I sat back, folding the knife I'd held to his throat when I first came into his plush condo.

I sighed. "You from California?"

He nodded.

"Like it here?"

He shook his head.

I smiled. "Probably a bad question right now, huh? Sorry."

He drooled.

"They don't do things in California the way they do things here, Mr. Knight. Do you understand that?"

He nodded.

A moment passed. "You must think I'm a bad person," I said.

He shook his head.

I looked away. The leather chair I sat in was incredibly comfortable. And besides the look of sheer terror on his face, the drool and the razor blades, it was almost like we were visiting.

There was a kind of peace here. The silence—the insulated walls and thick glass windows overlooking the city blocked out the noise I was used to. The yelling, honking and fighting of people crammed on top of each other like sardines was missing and, in this place, I could almost forget it was ever there.

I'd never sat in a chair as nice, let alone been inside such a plush place, and part of me hated him for it. I thought about my mom sitting in our dump of an apartment, drunk again on the couch, the vomit stain still on the carpet, and I never wanted to go back there, especially after being at Mr. Knight's.

Another moment passed and we stared at each other. For some reason, I wondered what he *really* thought of me.

I took a breath, looking around, then held up my knife. "My boss told me to cut you. Not a lot, but enough for you to understand what's going on. Enough to understand that you've made a mistake, and that you need to correct it."

His eye twitched.

I shook my head. "I think you're a decent guy, Mr. Knight. Actually, I'd bet you're a really nice man." I looked away, struggling with myself. "And that creates a problem for me, because usually the people I deal with aren't nice." I studied his face. "That makes it easier, you know? Most guys understand the game they're in, and so it's kind of like a 'buyer beware' kind of deal."

I inhaled slowly, looking into his eyes. "I'm not going to cut you, Mr. Knight, because I don't think you know what you signed on for when you moved here. So I'll be honest. South Boston is run by people you don't know. You don't know their names, what they look like, and you don't want to know them. Do you get that, Mr. Knight?"

He nodded.

I leaned forward. "Open your mouth." He hesitated, then opened up. I gently picked the blades off his tongue. "Tell me you are a man of your word."

"Please—don't hurt me. I'm begging you," he said, saliva trailing onto his sweater.

"Tell me, Mr. Knight. Are you an honest man?"

"Yes, I am."

I nodded. "Then I want you to give me your word that this zoning issue will be taken care of tomorrow."

He shuddered, his expression pained. "I can't promise—"

I didn't want to do it, but I had to, for his sake and for mine. I leaned forward, slapping his face hard. The crack echoed through the place. He grunted, openly sobbing now, his tears mixing with blood. If he didn't get the message, he'd be dead. And I didn't know if I could live with another death on my hands.

I clenched my teeth, angry at myself and the world and how it worked. "I'm not a bad person, Mr. Knight, but if you don't push that permit through, the man I work for will have you killed. And the man that will kill you enjoys hurting people. And the police that will investigate your death also work for my boss. That's how this game works." I said. "So I need your word, Mr. Knight, because I'm risking my life for you."

"I don't know what to do!" He cried. "I can't just switch things like that without suspicion and besides that I—"

I grabbed him by the shoulders, staring him in the face. "You want me to tell you what to do? Approve the zoning tomorrow, quit your job, and get on the first plane back to California. Because once you're in this game, you can't get out. And if you quit before approving the zoning, my boss will find you. Got it?"

He nodded.

"Give me your word: approval tomorrow."

He shuddered. "Yes. Okay. I promise."

I cut the binding from his wrists. "Shake on it, Mr. Knight," I said, holding out my hand.

He shook it. I swallowed. "You know that if you break your word, I'll be in trouble. I gave you a break here."

He wiped his mouth. "I understand."

I looked at him and I couldn't help but wonder again what he thought of me. "I'm not bad."

He said nothing.

I gestured to his condo. "You don't think I could ever have this, do you?"

His home was immaculate. Simple, uncluttered, with a few nice paintings on the walls, a big-screen television, leather sofas. Expensive.

"I don't know," he answered.

"Have you ever wanted something so bad, you'd do anything to get it?"

"I'm not sure what you're talking about."

I looked around. "How badly do you want this? What would you do to keep it? To get it if you didn't have it?"

His voice shook. "I suppose I'd work for it."

I studied his expression. "You've never been poor, have you?"

Silence.

"Have you ever eaten Salisbury steak?"

"No, I haven't."

"You'd know what I was talking about if you were ever poor."

He blinked and his shoulders relaxed just a bit. "You're young."

"Sixteen. Almost seventeen."

"You have a lot of time ahead of you."

I shook my head. "All I have is now, Mr. Knight. People with *things* have time. People with *nothing* only have now. But I'm not bad. It doesn't make me bad to get what I need."

"I believe you."

I stared at him. "You do, don't you?"

"Yes, I do."

"I'm sorry I busted your mouth."

He didn't answer.

I stood. "I think you are a nice person, Mr. Knight. But you're working with some not nice people, and they'll do anything to get what they need."

I stared at the blood on his sweater for a moment, thinking of Ben Capo with a plastic bag over his head. "They'll kill you, Mr. Knight. Believe me, they will."

Then I was gone.

chapter 22

I took the five hundred dollars I'd made from dealing with Mr. Knight and went to the Andrew Square Driving School, where I enrolled with a deposit of a hundred and twenty dollars. In three weeks' time, I'd have my license. I took the rest of the money and deposited three hundred of it into Mom's checking account to get ready for rent next month, and I spent the other eighty on a ring with a small diamond in it for Angel. I'd never in my life gone through money that fast.

The lady at the jewelry store smiled as she wrapped the little velour ring box and she told me that somebody would be very happy. I nearly told her I'd broken into a man's house and scared the shit out of him to get the money, but I thought it would ruin the moment.

As I walked out the door, I almost ran into my teacher, Mr. Langdon, who was just reaching for the door. I stopped. He looked at me and smiled. "Mr. O'Connor."

"Hello, Mr. Langdon."

He scratched behind his ear. "I've missed you in my class."

I looked away, uncomfortable with him uncomfortable. "If I go on school grounds, I get arrested."

"I heard about your...altercation."

I tensed up, the hackles on the back of my neck rising. "I fucked him up pretty good, if that's what you mean."

His eyes glinted and the touch of a smile crossed his lips. "I suppose you did. How are you doing, since 'fucking him up pretty good?'"

I studied him, not sure what his angle was. He said *fuck* like it was some foreign word, and I could tell he didn't use it often.

"I'm fine," I told him.

He nodded inside the jewelry store. "Doing some shopping?"

"Scoping the place out," I said.

He chuckled. "For an apparent robbery, I take it."

"Yeah."

He smiled, nodding to the bag in my hand. "Either love or Mother, I presume?"

I laughed. "Not *my* mother."

He paused, then looked at me, his eyes meeting mine. "I want you to know I met with the principal after you were expelled."

"Why?"

"I petitioned for your expulsion to be reduced to a suspension."

"Why?"

"Because I often disagree that the most troubled of our youth should be thrown out of the very thing that could save them."

I furrowed my brow. "I'm not troubled. And that school sucks."

He nodded again. "You really believe that, Aiden?"

I frowned. "You don't know shit about me."

"I know enough," he said, then stepped past me. As he did, he paused. "I wish you well, Mr. O'Connor."

I watched him go inside, not sure what had just happened. After walking down the street a ways, I stopped, turned around, and went back to the store, then leaned against the wall.

Mr. Langdon came out a few minutes later, walking away from me on the sidewalk. I followed him. "Mr. Langdon," I called.

He turned. "Yes?"

I caught up to him, stuffing my hands in my pockets. We faced each other, a question in his eyes. I wasn't sure what I wanted to say to him, but I knew I needed to say something.

"Thanks."

"For what?"

"For going to bat for me." I paused, then took a breath. "With me getting kicked out and all. I appreciate that."

"Well, you're welcome."

"Can I ask you a question?"

"Of course."

"Why did you give me that book? The one about boxing."

"As I said, I'm a teacher, and sometimes teaching means more than following policy."

"Yeah, I know, but why me?"

His eyes sharpened for a moment. "I knew you were interested in boxing."

I shook my head. "No. Why *me*? Why not somebody else? Half the school gets crappy grades, but you picked me. Why?"

He paused, thinking, then nodded. "Because I see potential in you, Aiden. But unfortunately, potential is neutral."

"What does that mean?"

"A person who has the potential to do great things also has the potential to do great harm." He tapped his head. "It's what we choose to do with our potential that matters."

"How do you decide, though? I mean, how do you know if what you choose is right?"

He smiled sadly. "Ah, the Golden Rule."

I looked at him, furrowing my brow.

"The Golden Rule. Do no harm to others so that they may do none to you."

I grunted. "That might be nice in *your* world, but that doesn't work in mine."

He shrugged. "It's universal, Aiden."

I looked at him, thinking of the bloody-mouthed zoning inspector, and my mother and Tommy, and just about everything else in my life.

"No, Mr. Langdon, it's not. Nothing is universal. Sometimes you have to hurt people to save them."

A long minute passed, then he said, "Can I help you with something, Aiden?"

111

I shook my head. "Every choice I have to make will hurt somebody."

He nodded. "The golden rule isn't a rule, really, Aiden. It's a goal. We're human, and humans hurt others. But striving toward what we know is right can alleviate the worst of the hurt."

chapter 23

Angel's father stood behind the counter of his pawn shop when I walked through the door. Slightly built and with fine features, he reminded me more of a darker Italian than a Cuban. He looked frail, tired and sick, with thinning hair and deep-set wrinkles in his face.

I walked to the counter, smiling. "Hello."

He nodded and smiled, his accent heavy. "What can I help you with, young man?"

"My name is Aiden O'Connor."

His expression went from that of a man looking at a customer to one of a father who didn't like what he was seeing.

"Yes," he said.

I held out my hand. "It's nice to meet you, Mr. Vives."

He didn't shake my hand.

I took a breath and he rested his weathered hands on the counter. Then he said "Yes?" once again.

"Is Angel here?"

"She is."

I waited. "May I see her, please?"

He raised his chin, looking down at me. "No, you may not."

I cleared my throat. "Why, sir?"

He glared. "I do not want my daughter to see you. I need no reason."

I deflated, not ready for another conflict. I decided my best bet was to be nice. "Angel tells me you're from Cuba."

He stared at me for a second, then nodded.

"I'd bet Cuba wasn't a very good place, huh? That's why you came here?"

He narrowed his eyes, and I half expected him to throw me out the door. But he answered me. "It is a different place. There is not opportunity there," he said stoically.

"Or freedom," I said.

His jaw muscles worked. "No, there is no freedom there."

I nodded. "So basically, you want to pull a Cuba on your daughter because I'm not 'right' for her. That's not fair, Mr. Vives. I just want to talk with her."

He studied me for a moment, then turned, walking through swinging doors to the back room. I heard voices in Spanish and, a moment later, Angel came out.

I smiled. "Hi."

Stress lined her face, but she smiled. "Hi. How are you?"

It'd been two days since we'd talked.

"Good. I enrolled in driving school," I told her.

She brightened. "I'm taking it this summer. My dad doesn't want me driving until I'm eighteen, but I got him to compromise. I'll get it six months sooner now."

"Cool. How was school today?"

She rolled her eyes. "Big test in chemistry."

"Pass?"

"I think so."

A moment passed, and the tension, at least in my head, was smothering me.

"I got you something," I told her.

She smiled, searching my face. "You did?"

I took the box from my jacket pocket and held it out.

She took it and smiled as she looked down at it.

"Go ahead. Open it."

She did, and when she lifted the lid, her eyes brightened. "Oh my god. Aiden…"

I grinned. "Like it? See the diamond? It's real. The lady said it's almost the best kind you can get."

She took the ring from the silk holder. "Aiden, how…."

I leaned over the counter and kissed her cheek. "I told you I can make you the queen of Southie."

She put it back, then closed the lid. "I can't take it, Aiden. I'm sorry."

"Why not?"

"Because it's too much. We're not even officially dating."

I nodded. "If we were dating, would you take it?"

She giggled. "You just won't give up, will you?"

"No."

"Well, then, yes. I would take it."

"Will you be my girlfriend?"

She smiled, but her eyes darkened. "Yes. But you have to ask my father."

"Why?"

"Tradition. I told you that's how he is."

"Okay, then. Take me to him."

"Aiden…"

I shrugged. "Take me to him. It'll be fine. I promise."

She said nothing for awhile, looking down at the box. Then she looked up and smiled. "All right, follow me."

We found Mr. Vives pricing DVDs on a shelf in the back. Angel stepped behind him and said, "Dad?"

He turned, frowning when he saw me.

I came forward. "I'd like to date your daughter. I know you don't like me because I'm white and I'm poor, but I really like Angel."

"You think I paddled from Cuba on a raft. I am a wetback, you say."

Oh shit. I glanced at Angel, then met his eyes. "I said that because I was angry at you."

"You are racist."

I set my jaw. "You are, too, sir."

He pursed his lips, nodded, then went on: "You have no money to take my daughter out to nice places."

"Yes, I do have money, Mr. Vives. I work."

"Do you steal?"

"No, I don't."

He nodded, thinking, then set his chin. "You may not date my daughter."

"I *will* date your daughter."

With that, he looked at Angel and let out a string of volatile Spanish words, waving his hands at me emphatically. She rested her hand on his arm, trying to calm him. A moment passed. He refused to look at me, turning back to the shelf.

Angel took my hand and led me out.

I sighed. "Sorry."

Of all things, she smiled. "He will like you. Don't worry."

I squinted at her. "What?"

She laughed. "Nobody has *ever* stood up to my father."

"So?"

She squeezed my hand. "So I like that. He will, too. Just give him some time to come around."

"You have a weird way of doing things, you know that?" I said.

She rolled her eyes. "And you don't? At least I don't beat guys up."

Then it hit me. "We're dating?"

She grinned. "Yes, Aiden, we are."

I left the store with my heart pounding and my ring on her finger.

chapter **24**

Two days later, I opened our apartment door after I was done with my driving class to find Mom sitting at the kitchen table with Conor. She'd made herself up, putting on a decent outfit and of course she was drunk, but at least she wasn't sloppy. I glanced at the dirty dishes in the sink and the half-eaten soggy bowl of cereal on the counter from that morning.

"What are you doing here?" I asked Conor.

He stood. "What's up, kiddo? I just stopped by to say hello."

"Why?"

Mom interrupted. "Conor says you've quit boxing. You haven't been to the gym, Aiden?"

"No."

Her eyes were on fire. "First you get kicked out of school, then you're gone at all hours, and now…"

I ignored her, staring at Conor. "Don't come here."

"I just came to see you."

"You heard me," I said, looking around in shame.

He took his coat from the back of the chair as Mom glared at me. "Aiden O'Connor, you will not be rude to guests in this house!"

"It's not a house. It's a shitty apartment, and you're drunk." I turned to him. "You're not welcome here. Leave." I opened the door, waiting for him.

He nodded, said goodbye to my mother, then walked out. I followed him into the hall. "Why'd you come here?" I asked.

He turned, the calm before my storm. "Why? I just came to…"

I clenched my teeth, interrupting. "Stay out of our business."

His face went flat, his expression hard. "I got out of your business a long time ago, Aiden."

"What is that supposed to mean?"

"It means you're fucking up your life. I came here to help you, and your mother is an old friend."

"Oh, yeah? How can you help me? By busting my balls every time you see me? You're not my father, man. My father is gone. Long gone." I pointed to the door. "And she is, too, so mind your business, okay? I've got enough crap to deal with already, without you giving me shit, too."

A silence passed between us, then he nodded. "Fair enough. Be at the gym at five tomorrow. Without the mouth, because if you speak this way in my gym, I'll shove my fist down your throat."

I blinked. "What?"

He turned away. "You heard me. I've lined up a sparring match for you."

I furrowed my brow. "I just told you—"

"I know. Your business is your business. But you can fight. No more hassle. My word."

Then he turned and walked away.

chapter 25

Tommy and Liam sat at the card table in the back room of the pub when I walked in, and Lilly was sitting at his usual spot on the couch. Another man sat at the table, one I'd never seen before. At around forty-five years old, olive-skinned, dressed in a fine suit and tie to match, and with a sharp haircut, he reminded me of a rich lawyer or businessman.

He clasped his hands on the table, diamond-studded rings on each long, slender middle finger. When he looked at me, his jaw muscles tightened. Liam nodded toward the empty chair. "Have a seat, Aiden."

I did, and Lilly sat up, his eyes going from the television to the table.

Something was up and I didn't like it.

Liam slid his chair back a bit, then crossed his ankle over his knee. "We've got a small issue, Aiden."

The man shook his head slowly. "Not a small issue, sir."

Liam nodded. "Not a small issue, then. An issue."

I looked at Tommy and he shifted in his seat. A pistol in his waistband caught my eye. I clenched my teeth.

"What issue?" I asked them.

Liam went on. "The young man you had a conflict with at school a few days ago is the nephew of a business partner of mine from Roxbury." He nodded to the man. "Mr. Lorenzo represents this partner."

I looked at the man and nodded.

He didn't nod back, but spoke directly to Liam. "I'm sure there will be a resolution to this problem, yes?"

Liam nodded, glancing at Lilly, who stood, walked over to a cabinet, opened it up, and took out three stacks of hundred-dollar bills. He brought them to the table and set them in front of Liam, then returned to his place on the couch.

Liam cleared his throat. "We would take care of any medical bills, along with a gift to his family. This was obviously a mistake, and Aiden wishes to apologize."

Liam's eyes met mine in a flat and level stare.

Time passed, our eyes locked, and I knew I was treading on dangerous territory. At least fifteen thousand dollars were stacked on the table. I swallowed, keeping my attention on Liam. "I didn't know he was connected. I apologize."

With that, Mr. Lorenzo reached for a soft leather briefcase, opened it in his lap and put the money inside. Then he clasped it shut, saying, "My boss would like more."

A tension filled the room. Liam uncrossed his legs and sat straight. Lilly cleared his throat and got up from the couch. Tommy lowered his right hand from the table, hooking his thumb in his waistband next to the pistol.

Liam exhaled. "Give me terms," he said at last.

He nodded. "We would like to see disciplinary action taken. For us to continue our business relationship, an example needs to be set," he said, looking me up and down. "It cannot be allowed that any individual would think it acceptable to behave in such a way."

A long moment passed and Liam's eyes never left mine. Then he leaned forward, his back straight as a rod, as he rested his forearms on the table. "You tell Mr. Jimenez that I handle what goes on in my organization in my own way. Measures have been taken. It will not happen again."

"We would like to know what measures have been taken."

In a flash, Liam was up, knocking the chair over as he pulled a revolver from behind his back. He put it against Mr. Lorenzo's temple, cocking it. His voice was low and deep as he spoke slowly.

"I don't think that Mr. Jimenez would appreciate having your dead body dumped on his front steps due to a mistake in *your* judgment, would he? You get my drift?"

The man swallowed. "Yes."

"Would you like to question my word again that measures have been taken to make sure this will not happen again?"

"No, sir, I wouldn't."

"Would you like to disrespect my people again?"

"No."

"Good," Liam told him. "Then we have an agreement." He kept the pistol cocked and against Lorenzo's head. "And, as an act of good faith, we'll include a three-percent payment increase in the next shipment. Are we clear?"

"Yes."

Liam took the pistol away and sat down, waving the gun at the door. "Good," he said. "Now get out."

Silence fell over the room after Lorenzo left. Liam pursed his lips and spoke to me.

"You know what just happened here, don't you?"

I nodded. "Yes."

"The only reason you're still sitting in that chair is because I like you, Aiden."

My insides quivered. "I didn't know who he was."

"I know. And I don't need to tell you how much money I just spent to keep you alive."

"No, you don't."

He stood, walking to a cupboard on the far wall, taking out a bottle of Irish whiskey. He poured a bit into a tumbler, drank it, put the bottle back, then turned to me.

"Lilly, Tommy, give Aiden and me a few minutes."

Both got up and left.

Liam sat down. "You don't owe me anything for that."

I stared at him, waiting for his angle to come out. Nothing came free in Southie.

He smiled. "You don't believe me, do you?"

"No."

He nodded. "You have potential, Aiden. Great potential. You're smart, tough, and more than anything, you're not afraid to stand up for what you think is right. I look for that in people. People with principles and loyalties they won't budge on. I just invested in that by paying them."

"Even if my principles are against you?"

He laughed. "You're not against me, Aiden. You're against yourself, and I know you'll come to see that." He paused, then went on. "The only reason you're here is because you love your mother. You'll sacrifice yourself for her and I appreciate that. But you don't have to sacrifice; you have what it takes to be great. To be rich. And I can help you be that."

"Maybe," I said.

He shook his head. "No, Aiden, you do. I know you think I'm a thug and a crook, but it's never that simple. Life is never black and white. I keep things good in Southie. I keep streets safe and people secure," he told me.

Then he waved to the door. "That gentleman, Mr. Lorenzo, works for a man who'd tear Southie apart if I wasn't here to prevent it. He doesn't care about us or what we do, or how the good people here live. He'd let it rot as long as he made money. His boys would destroy this place. But I'm not that way. I care. I keep us safe from people like them. They're outsiders."

I took a breath. It was Liam's version of the golden rule. Obviously, my teacher Mr. Langdon didn't know squat about Southie.

"Would you have killed him?" I asked Liam.

"He questioned my word," he told me.

I didn't know what to say and it showed.

Liam patted the table. "You just think about what I said, Aiden. Take a day or so. Think about what you want in this life and maybe I could help you get it. Maybe we can help each other."

"I will—I'll think about it."

"I know you will, and that's why you have a future."

I stood up from my seat. "I've got to go."

He smiled. "Sure. You take it easy, huh?"

I reached the door, and as I turned the handle, Liam called my name. I turned. "Yeah?"

"Tell your mother she has a job at The Quencher Tavern down on I Street. She starts tomorrow. Eight to twelve shift."

I stared at him.

"No strings attached, Aiden. My word."

"Okay," I said.

He smiled, then, and spoke. "By the way, you did a great job with that Mr. Knight guy. Got the zoning the next morning."

"Cool. Glad he's on board," I said, relieved.

Liam laughed. "He's not on board. He quit the next day. Back to California, I guess." He studied me. "You must have done a number on him, huh?"

I shrugged. "I guess so."

chapter 26

All the usual sights, smells, noises and people were there, but things were different this time when I stepped into the ring. I glanced to the side, where Angel stood, her arms crossed, nervous in a sea of sweaty guys. She forced a smile when she saw me looking at her and I smiled back, raising a glove.

When I told her I'd be sparring today she'd wanted to come. We had something in common as we stepped through the doors; I was nervous, too.

Conor let me know that Kelso Giambi, the guy in the ring who I was about to spar with, had fought his first pro bout just a week ago. He'd won by decision in four rounds. Taller by two inches, he outweighed me by five pounds, had a longer reach and looked like a solid band of muscle. He was also twenty-three years old.

As I adjusted my headgear, Conor called out to us. "No holding back, guys. Keep it clean, hard, and have fun." Then he rang the bell.

His first shot didn't hurt so much as it surprised me. Blindingly quick, he snaked his fist through my guard like thread through a needle and jabbed me straight in the face, following up with a left that grazed my headgear, then coming in hard to the body.

The guy danced back, bouncing on the balls of his feet before surprising me again with a lunge and a right to the head that made my ears ring.

"Too slow, Aiden! Guard up, guard up! Move around him!" Conor yelled.

My stomach was fluttering faster than Kelso's fists came at me, jab after jab, and suddenly I didn't want Angel here—not now. I could face a gym full of guys in a real match and be fine, but not this; not when I hadn't even landed a punch on this guy. He was more like a ghost than some Italian guy from 3rd Street with mallets for hands.

After another few seconds of pounding, Conor rang the bell early and called me over. "If you don't *think* you can hit him, you *won't* hit him. If you don't *think* you can win, you won't. If you don't *think* you can do this, you can't. Now get in there and show yourself that you can, Aiden."

So I got back into the ring, Conor rang the bell, and I studied Kelso. He rotated clockwise, and every time he threw a heavy right, he dropped his left to his waist, exposing himself as he stepped back. The next time he tried it, I drove in to pound his ribs with everything I had, starting off with a hard right, followed by four jabs to his midsection and ending with a wicked uppercut to his chin—my bread-and-butter punch.

When you hit a guy, he doesn't need to make a sound for you to know he's hurt, and I knew I'd hurt him. He danced back to break but I didn't let him, pounding his face with a combination that took him to the ropes.

I knew he'd try to clinch, coming in from the ropes and getting inside my punches. So when he did, instead of sliding away, I landed a left to his shoulder that sent him reeling backward and I closed in again, this time pummeling his midsection to the sound of air being forced from his lungs.

My arms screamed with fatigue and my lungs ached; everything in me said to back off and regroup, but I didn't. I couldn't—I had this guy if my body didn't give out. So I kept on him, his back against the ropes as I punched him down the line and into the corner—the sweet spot.

Kelso held on with a weak guard and I concentrated on his head, batting his gloves away and landing him with sweeping strikes. Finally, he hunched over and lowered his chin to protect his face. I had about one second so I went for it; I stepped back, lowered my center of balance, and threw the hardest uppercut I had in me. With his chin down, I caught him square on the nose and he crumpled, dazed as he landed on his butt.

Conor rang the bell.

With Kelso groggy on the mat, I looked up and realized the gym was silent. Every eye was on the ring—on me. On us.

Danny MacDonald, who'd been working the speed bag across the gym but had stopped to watch the end of the match, shook his head and shouted, "Looks like you've got one hell of a kid on your hands, Conor," his voice echoing across the place.

Conor stared at me with a huge grin. "You bet your ass I do, Danny!" he called.

Kelso began to rise and I helped him up, both of us awkward in our gloves. He breathed deep. "Nice," he said. Then he left the ring without another word, heading toward the locker room.

I looked at Angel, who stood there, her eyes wide and her mouth set like she'd just seen an alien. Then she grinned and began to laugh—it was the sweetest sound I'd ever heard.

I'd just TKO'd a pro with headgear, and I couldn't believe it.

Conor couldn't, either. He took us to his office, where Angel and I sat as Conor cut the tape from my wrists.

"Damn!" he said.

"What?" I asked him.

He laughed. "Nothing."

"What, Conor?"

He bent to his task, stripping tape away. "I thought we'd bring Kelso in to show you what it's like, you know? Show you that you could stand up to a pro."

"So you didn't think I'd win?"

He chuckled. "Hell, no. He's a pro. Been training for years to get there."

I laughed. "So you set me up to lose?"

"No. I set you up to prove what you could do."

I breathed. "So, now what?"

He finished with the tape, put the scissors in his desk and sat. "So now we get you your first pro fight."

I looked at him. "You're crazy, right? You don't just go

pro, do you? Shouldn't I go after the title for the New England Lowell Golden Gloves Tournament or something?"

He shrugged. "You're not normal, kid. I think you can do it, and I don't care how you're *supposed* to do things."

"Don't I need a management contract?"

He laughed. "One step at a time. Win the first fight."

"Got anybody in mind?"

He nodded. "There's a kid up north from New Hampshire I've been hearing about. Nineteen, your weight. Won three, lost three. I think he'd be a good match."

"Cool."

He nodded. "You almost ran out of steam in there."

"Yeah."

"How much you run?"

"I try for three miles every other day."

"You need more cardio. You've got the power and the fists, but you need stamina."

"Okay."

"Plan on around three weeks for the fight to be set."

"That soon?"

He smiled. "You can do it, Aiden. The kid I'm thinking about goes for big stuff. He can hit, but you can wear him down. You're quick, and those body shots did Kelso in."

"I thought the face shots did it."

He shook his head. "They hurt him, but if a guy can't catch his breath, he gets weak." He chuckled. "Lack of oxygen tends to make people fall down."

"You look nice."

"Thank you," she replied.

chapter 27

The bathroom door was open and Mom leaned over the sink in front of the mirror, applying mascara. She hadn't taken a drink all day, and her hands trembled just the slightest. Ever since she'd cut her head on the table, she'd toned down the drinking, even walking to the grocery store instead of leaving it to me.

"Your shift starts at eight?" I asked.

She nodded, dabbing her eyelashes. "I'll be home by twelve-thirty. And no going out for you."

I looked at her. "Nervous?"

She put the cap on the mascara. "One bar is the same as the next."

I leaned against the doorjamb. "I met a girl."

She stopped. "Who?"

"Her name is Angel."

She smiled. "Angel. That's a pretty name."

I hesitated. "I'd like you to meet her."

She nodded. "We'll have her over for dinner my first day off."

I swallowed. "I was thinking I could bring her by the Quencher tonight. We were going to meet anyway."

"I said no going out tonight."

It almost popped out of my mouth that the only time she gave a crap was when she was sober, and the last time she'd been sober was weeks ago. "Please? Just for milkshakes and stopping by to say hi. I'll be home by ten."

She set her mouth. "Is this place not good enough for her?"

I shuffled. "No, Mom. That's not it. The Quencher's on the way and I thought it would be nice for you to see her."

She thought for a moment. "Okay. But I'll only have a minute. First night on the job and all."

"When is your break? Maybe then would be good."

She dug in her purse, taking out her schedule. "It's at ten."

"Then can I be home at ten-thirty? That way we can drop by on your break."

"Okay," she said, hesitating. "So, tell me again how you found out about this job?"

"I did some stuff for the owner," I lied. "He was hiring, so I got you an interview."

She smirked. "I told you, no jobs. And I appreciate you putting money in the account, but we had a deal."

I smiled. *Funny how money in the bank calms the situation down.* Sure, she didn't want me working, but not enough to press it when I was putting hundreds in the account. "It's not a job, really. Just doing odd stuff here and there," I said, hovering right on the edge of the truth.

"You need to go to school, Aiden."

I laughed. "Sort of hard to do if you get arrested for stepping foot on school property."

She grunted. "I know. I'm working on that."

I sighed. *Oh boy.*

chapter 28

The Quencher Tavern was nicer than most of the other places Mom had worked, and as Angel and I stood outside, I looked at the polished brass door handles and exhaled.

Angel took my hand in hers. "You're nervous, aren't you?"

I nodded. "Yeah."

She giggled. "Just because I'm not Catholic and Irish and white?"

I laughed. "Yeah, pretty much. But I want her to meet you."

"Our parents make quite a pair, huh?" she said.

"They sure do."

She squeezed my hand. "Well, if you can meet my father, I can meet your mother. We can be a team."

I smiled. "Yeah. The odd couple."

"Screw them, anyway," she said.

I looked at her, surprised. "Wow."

She shrugged. "You were right, Aiden. We're together for the right reasons, and letting the wrong reasons get in the way would be stupid. I like you."

I wanted to tell her right then and there that I loved her. I'd blurt it out to the world and not care if Southie liked it or not. But I couldn't. Something inside told me I'd look like a fool if I did. Besides, could you love somebody only after a few weeks? Was it puppy love? Stupid love? I'd never even had a girlfriend before. I was insane to even think about saying that to her now.

I led her to the doors. "Well, come on then. I know she'll love you." I smiled. "Who couldn't love you?"

I led her inside and asked for Mrs. O'Connor. Soon, Mom came from the back. When she saw Angel, she stopped. Her eyes went to our clasped hands. Her mouth snapped shut. I swallowed hard. "Hi, Mom."

She exhaled. "I only have a minute."

Angel held out her hand and Mom shook it. Angel took a breath. "It's nice to meet you, Mrs. O'Connor," she said, smiling.

Mom eyed me. "Yes, it certainly is." She paused. "So…how long have you two been seeing each other?"

Angel smiled. "Well, I guess officially only a few days."

Mom nodded. "I've not seen you at the parish."

"I'm not Catholic, ma'am," Angel said.

Dead silence from my mom.

I cut in. "Angel's father owns the pawn shop at Perkin's Square. Cool, huh? You should see all the amazing stuff in there."

Mom nodded. "Wonderful. How long have you been in America?"

"Twelve years. I was four when we moved from Cuba to Florida."

"You speak American well."

Angel smiled, throwing me a quick glance. "Thank you. My father enrolled me in English courses as soon as we arrived in the States. He insisted we speak the language."

"Angel is an honor student," I said, beaming. "Straight A's."

My mother smiled. "Well, that's just great for you. I've got to get back now." She turned to me. "Aiden, be home by ten-thirty. No later." She turned back to Angel. "It was nice meeting you."

Then she was gone, back to the bar.

Outside, we walked in silence for half a block. Then she giggled. "You could just tell how much she loved me."

"I'm sorry."

She shook her head. "Don't be. We're a team, remember?"

I laughed. "Yeah."

"And at least I speak American well."

"Hey now…"

"I know, Aiden. It's just funny."

"She didn't graduate high school."

She stopped, smiling. "If I can't make a joke about your mom after you call my father a raft-paddling wetback, we've got a problem."

I rolled my eyes. "Thanks for the reminder."

"You're welcome." She leaned over and kissed me.

"It'll be a long time before you live that one down, you racist."

"A long time, huh?"

She smiled demurely. "Maybe, freckles. Maybe."

◆

We walked along Carson Beach on the way back to her apartment and found a bench near the Soda Shack. Sitting in the moonlight, we kissed for awhile, her breath sweet and the taste of her mouth like heaven; her body melted into mine like warm butter.

Then she broke away and we sat for a moment. I held her hand. "What's wrong?" I asked.

"What are you going to do, Aiden?"

"About what?"

"About…I guess about you. About us."

"What do you mean?"

"I mean school. And boxing."

"I'm going pro. You heard Conor."

"Yeah, but what about after that? You said your mom didn't graduate. What about you?"

I shrugged. "I can go pro, Angel. I can do it."

"I know, but what about an alternate plan? Shouldn't you at least get back in school? What if boxing doesn't work out?"

I smiled, kissing her neck. "It will. I promise. And I promised to make you the queen of Southie."

She pulled away. "Yeah, but…"

"But what? I don't need school. And besides, I'm expelled. I can't go back."

She shook her head. "You can petition the district, and even if they don't accept you, you can still go to another district."

"Why? I'm making money now, and I'll start making money with bouts, too. I'm going places, Angel. I am. You'll see."

She squeezed my hand. "I know, but I just think it would be good to finish school, you know? Just as something to fall back on."

"School is stupid."

She looked at her lap. "No, it's not."

I smiled, squeezing her hand. "Well, it's not for you, but for me it is."

"I wish you'd think about it."

"Why?"

She turned, facing me. "Aiden, do you know why I'm here?"

"Yeah. Because America rocks."

She nodded. "My father came here so I could go to school. So I could do what he couldn't do in his own country."

I cleared my throat. "I know, and that's cool. But Southie is different. It's not like Cuba."

"You're right. It's not like Cuba. We have choices here."

I stopped, letting the words sink in. Then I thought about Mr. Langdon and his Golden Rule. "Maybe so," I said.

"I know so, Aiden."

"So you're giving me some kind of ultimatum, then?"

"No. I'd just like you to think about it," she said.

I leaned over, kissing her, then whispered in her ear. "I will, okay? I promise." I laughed softly. "But I've got to focus on smashing people in the ring for now."

"I still think you should get back in school."

"You're always so serious about everything," I said.

She smiled. "I have to be. I remember a little bit of Cuba. We lived in a house with no electricity before my mom died."

"Wow."

"Yeah. So I have to plan things, you know? And my dad is sick, Aiden. Very sick."

"What're you saying?"

"I'm saying he probably won't be here by the time I graduate." She faltered, looking away. "I have to plan for that."

"I'll take care of you."

She kissed me again. "I know. But I have to take care of myself, first."

I understood that. I always had. And I knew that if anybody was meant for me, it was Angel. I didn't care if I was a fool for feeling the way I did after such a short time.

"Yeah," I said. "I know. But I can help."

As we sat on the bench and talked about how she felt about her father dying, I caught a glimpse of two figures coming toward us on the walkway. I tensed and she looked at me.

"What?" she said.

I kept my eyes on them. "Nothing. Just getting late, is all. I'd better get you home," I said, standing.

"Aiden…."

I took her hand. "Come on. Let's go."

The two men picked up their pace. Angel looked at me. "Aiden, what's happening?"

"This way," I said, taking her at a fast pace from the beach in the direction of Columbus Park.

She looked over her shoulder. "Aiden, they're following us—"

We passed a garbage bin and I reached in, picking up a glass soda bottle. "When I say so, I want you to run as fast as you can, understand? Go straight home, and don't call the police."

She pulled against me. "Aiden, you're scaring me."

I glanced over my shoulder. They were gaining on us. "I know you're scared, but do as I say. Just do it, okay, Angel? I'll tell you about it later."

"Aiden, tell me now—"

I squeezed her hand. "You have to *run*. Now GO!" I said, pulling away from her and turning around.

The two men were thirty yards away, but when they saw me face them, they slowed.

Angel stood there, frozen. "Go!" I insisted, my breath coming in short bursts.

At last, Angel ran down the hill and I stood my ground. One of the men bolted after her, splitting off from his buddy. My heart sank and I screamed for her to run as I raised the empty bottle and let fly with it. From ten feet away, the man coming for me didn't have time to dodge. And as the glass hit his mouth, I heard the crack of teeth on glass.

I didn't wait to see if he'd fallen and sprinted down the hill, watching as Angel fled into the trees. The man was following, gaining on her, his legs going like pistons. Angel cut to the right and the man followed, their two shadows zigzagging under the trees. I cut diagonally across a small grassy area, my lungs pumping as hard as my legs until I came between the two running shadows.

When I was a body-length from the guy, I dove, wrapping my arms around his legs like a linebacker. He fell flat, skidding on his face in the grass as I rolled and got back to my feet. He turned on his back, frantically digging in his coat pocket for something, his dark eyes on me. But before he could get his hand out, I drove the toe of my sneaker into his crotch. With a low and painful grunt, he curled up in a ball and rocked back and forth, moaning.

I glanced back, and the other guy, no doubt minus a few teeth, staggered after us. I didn't wait—I took off running and followed Angel as she disappeared into the darkness. Moments later, I caught up to her, falling in beside her as she ran.

She was crying and winded, her chest heaving as she wracked out sobs.

"Follow me," I said, grabbing her hand.

We raced across the park, then hit the street where I yanked Angel back and out of the path of an oncoming car.

The projects were close and I thought we could make

it there if we were lucky, so we ran. Angel was slowing and I squeezed her hand, pulling her along, my own lungs burning as we sprinted across Columbia Road and bolted into an alcove leading to some basement stairs.

In the darkness, the only sound was our breathing. Angel held back sobs and I put my finger to my lips in the dim light. "Shhh. They won't find us here. It'll be okay."

She nodded, but it wasn't okay. Nothing was okay. Minutes passed, and as our breathing slowed and the rustling of rats running along the pipes overhead sent shivers up my spine, all I could say was that I was sorry.

She sniffed.

"You want me to tell you what's going on?"

She shook her head. "I already know."

"You know what?"

"I know how you make money, Aiden. And this has something to do with it."

My breath caught. "No—I mean, yes—but those guys weren't after me because of what I do."

"I don't believe you."

I clenched my teeth, frustrated. "I'm not a liar, Angel. I would never lie to you."

She looked away. "I don't want to know. I want you to go back to school. I want to be with you and I want everything to be normal."

"No, it's not about what you think. It's about Mark Thomason—when I punched his throat. Remember?"

She swallowed. "Yes. How could I forget?"

"Well, he's connected to a guy in Roxbury. Now they're after me."

She looked down.

"I'm not lying."

A moment passed and she looked into the darkness. "I need to go home, Aiden," she said. "My father will worry."

I peeked out and could see nothing but the shadow of an old drunk staggering home after a heavy night of drinking.

"Okay," I told her. "Come on."

chapter 29

After dropping Angel off at her door, I stood across the street in the shadows of an alley, watching for ten minutes. Not a person in sight. Feeling certain that we hadn't been followed, I jogged down the alley, then made a beeline to Liam's condominium in Thomas Park, which overlooked the city lights.

I'd never been there before and it was known that knocking on his door for any reason was off limits. But I didn't care. I knocked, rang and knocked again. A minute later, he swung the door open and I had the barrel of a huge pistol in my face. He looked me up and down, then looked behind me, still not lowering the piece.

"Get in here," he said.

With the pistol still aimed at me, I went inside. He shut the door, then ushered me through the living room and into a small closet with a thick glass door. He opened it and I was greeted with the sweet and thick smell of cigars. I glanced at the boxes on small shelves as he shut the door, sealing us in. He sat on a stool, the pistol dangling in his hand as he hooked a bare foot on a rung.

"This place is soundproof and vacuum sealed. I check for microphones every day." He stared at me as I breathed in the aromas. "Now talk," he said.

I told him what happened.

"Shit," he said.

"What's going on? I thought everything was taken care of."

He took a breath, then spoke. "I'll take care of it."

"How? You already tried, Liam, and I'm not doubting you, but—"

He leveled his eyes on me. "I said I'll take care of it, Aiden."

I swallowed, a million questions running through my mind.

"You can't go home," he told me.

I stared at him.

"They know where you live."

"What about—"

He took a phone from his robe pocket and dialed. "Yeah. It's me. Put two of your guys outside The Quencher. Have them tail the O'Connor woman home, then watch over the place. Yeah. She lives in the projects. And I don't want her knowing she's being followed."

Then he hung up, looking at me. "This will take some time, Aiden. A day. Maybe two." He eyed me. "This girl special to you?"

I nodded.

"Then you can't see her."

I said nothing.

He shook his head, standing. "If you give a shit about

that girl, Aiden, you won't set eyes on her again until this blows over. Got it?"

I nodded. "Yes."

"Go to the pub. Lilly will meet you there. You'll stay at his place."

I rolled my eyes. "Lilly doesn't like me, Liam. Maybe I should—"

His neck flushed and he clenched his teeth. "You have anything else you want to give me advice on, Aiden?" He sat down, gesturing at me.

"Go ahead. Why don't you tell me how to run my business, huh? I'm sure you've got a ton of advice on how to live in a shitty hole with two drunks for parents."

His eyes drilled into me. "Go ahead. I'm listening."

I swallowed, my cheeks burning as I glanced at the pistol in his hand. "I didn't mean it that way."

"Lesson number one: Keep your fucking mouth shut unless you have something to say. Got it?"

"Yes."

He shook his head, gesturing to the open slider door. "Get out."

chapter 30

Lilly looked like a fat warthog ready to rip my guts out. He sat on the couch in the back room, his hair messed up and sleep in his eyes. I closed the door behind me and said hi.

He stood, pulling up his belt. "We ain't roomies. You just remember that when I take you to my place. Keep your hands to yourself and don't mess nothing up. Now let's go."

We walked outside, where he opened the door of a late-model Cadillac. I'd seen it parked there before. I opened the passenger door and hopped in. He fired up the engine and put it in gear. I leaned my head back on the head rest. "This sucks."

"You're a winner, kid," he growled.

"They'll be even more pissed now."

"Well, they come to my door and I'll hand your ass over on a platter."

I looked over at him. "You've had something against me since the day we met."

"I got something against everybody."

"No, you don't. You don't like me. Why?"

He grunted. "What, are you Dr. fucking Phil now? I don't like you because I don't like you. So keep your mouth shut before I slap you like your mother does."

I rolled my eyes. "Sure."

He glanced at me, pissed off. "Go ahead. Test me."

"Go to hell, Lilly."

He slammed on the brakes, stopping in the middle of the road. Then his pistol was in my face. "I said, don't test me," he snarled.

I yawned. "Testing, one, two, three." Our eyes met and seconds passed.

It was the second gun in my face that night and I was getting tired of it. "Liam pulls every string you got, so put the gun away and drive."

His eyes bulged and I knew that he would have sold his own mother to shoot me, but he couldn't.

"I said drive, Lilly."

He did. After a few minutes, he broke the silence. "You'd better watch your back."

"I'm getting used to that."

He laughed. "Yeah, you think you got power, but you don't. You don't know shit about what's going on, and I ain't just talking about that punk you beat up."

"There's more to it than the kid I punched?"

He laughed. "Hell, yeah. At least to Liam there is."

"What is it?"

He glanced at me, a sly smile coming to his face. "Why don't you just go ask your old man about that, huh? Maybe he'll take you out for ice cream and a ball game, too."

"What does my father have to do with this?"

For awhile he said nothing. Then, in the stillness of the car, he told me. "You gotta' be out of your head to think a man like Liam would waste a red cent on a kid like you unless there was a reason."

chapter 31

I slept on Lilly's couch, and he would say no more about my dad or why Liam was protecting me. I couldn't even get a blanket out of the guy, let alone answers, so when I woke up, I headed straight for the door.

Lilly looked up from eating a piece of cold fried chicken for breakfast. "You ain't leavin'," he said, smacking his lips.

"Yeah, I am."

He shook his head, chomping away. "No, you ain't. Liam's got to take care of business to save your soft little ass from the big bad men."

"Are you ever in a good mood?"

"Not with you around."

"Your mother dropped you on your head, didn't she?" I said.

"Funny," he said, licking grease from his fingers. "You should be a comedian."

"I'm leaving."

He shrugged. "It's your ass."

I watched him eat for a moment longer, then opened the door. "Yeah, it is."

◆

I started with his oldest haunt, a pool hall and bar across town. The bartender was mopping the floor of the empty place when I walked in. He glanced at me. "We're open, but you ain't of age. Find the door."

"I'm Aiden O'Connor."

He stopped mopping, then smiled. "Hell, yeah. Nick's boy—the boxer. He talks you up all the time."

I gaped. *My dad talked me up?* I let that sink in for a second, "You know where he is?"

He laughed. "Yeah, I know, because I put him there last night."

"Where?"

"Jail."

I stared at him, confused.

He grinned, shaking his head. "It ain't that way, kid. He gets into his liquor a bit too much sometimes and causes trouble. So we got an agreement: I call the cops before he starts busting stuff up besides heads and lips, and they haul him away. Saves me money buying new furniture. He gets sober, he's welcome to come back when he gets out."

He held out his hand. "Name is Jay. Your dad and I go back."

I shook. "He's down at the station, huh?"

He nodded. "It's a hundred-thirty-dollar bail for public drunkenness. I usually pay it, then he pays me back when he gets his check."

"You don't have to this time. I need to talk to him."

He looked me up and down. "You got a hundred thirty?"

"I work."

He chuckled. "Good for you, kid." He paused. "You got any matches coming up? I read about the amateur title."

I smiled. "Yeah. First pro match'll be soon."

"When?"

"Not sure."

He nodded. "I'll hear about it. Conor comes in every once in awhile."

"Conor? From the gym?"

He laughed. "'Course. We all go back. School and such."

◆

I passed the welcome sign in front of the impressive brick façade of the South Boston Police Department, complete with pretty shrubs and flowers surrounding it, and couldn't help but laugh to myself. "Welcome" to cops meant "Put your hands behind your head and spread your feet."

Inside, I walked up to the counter where a pudgy, dark-haired cop in his forties dutifully ignored me, chin down, reading a newspaper. I stared at the top of his head and cleared my throat.

He looked up, snapping the paper shut. "Yeah?"

"I need to bail out my dad. Where do I go?"

He looked me up and down. "Shouldn't you be in school? I could write you up for delinquency."

"I was expelled."

He grunted. "Figures. What, you hit a teacher or something?"

I shook my head, smiling. "Naw. I hit a desk cop. Where do I go?"

He furrowed his brow. "Don't be a fresh prick with me." Then he jabbed a finger toward a hall. "Down there."

I followed his directions and eventually found the lady I needed to see, signed the papers and forked over the money as she eyed me suspiciously. She finally couldn't keep the cork in her mouth any longer. "That sure is a lot of money for a boy your age to have."

"I beat up people for the Mafia. It pays well."

She stared at me for a moment, then grinned. "Your mother sent you, huh?"

"Sure. Where do I get him?"

She told me, so I moved along to the next office, showed the papers to another officer in a cage and waited. Fifteen minutes later, my dad was escorted through a door by a monster of a cop. I got to my feet and my dad stopped walking and stared at me.

Then he grunted, looked to his left, went to the cage to get his personal belongings, which consisted of a billfold, watch, a ring, a dime and two crumpled dollar bills.

The officer told my dad not to spend it all in one place,

and my dad told him to go to hell. Both officers laughed. I faced my father when he turned away from the cage.

A moment passed, his eyes searching mine before he shrugged. "Why aren't you in school?" he asked me.

"Expelled."

Anger flashed in his eyes and his lips thinned. "You—"

"We need to talk," I said.

His face could have been a thunderstorm. I'd never spoken to him like this before and he didn't like it one bit. "We need to talk when I got something to say," he said, then began walking toward the door.

I followed. "Old hat at this, huh?"

"Shut the fuck up," he said, glancing over his shoulder.

"Your buddy at the bar told me about your agreement."

We exited the building and reached the sidewalk. Then he turned, grabbed a fistful of my shirt and twisted it tight. His breath was stale and rancid.

"Watch your mouth around me," he said.

"Tell me about Liam."

The world froze for an instant, his face inches from mine. Then he let go and walked away.

I called after him.

He turned, his slacks and shirt crumpled from sleeping in a cell. "I ain't got nothing to say, kid. Mind your business."

Then he turned away again.

"It *is* my business."

He raised his voice, not bothering to turn. "You're a damn fool if it is."

I thought about what to say but couldn't come up with anything, so I watched him walk away, the sun reflecting on his greasy hair and that swagger I knew him by just a little bit defeated. Then I went home, not sure if I was happy I'd stood up to him or a damn fool for trying.

◆

"You can start by telling me why you didn't come home last night, and you can also explain why two men followed me home after work and have been milling around the entrance to our building all day long."

I looked at my mom. She stood at the stove, stirring a pot of soup and sipping from a tumbler. Above her, on the shelf, was a bottle of whiskey with felt-marker lines on it. "I stayed at Tommy's. He needed help with his mom."

"Liar."

A few seconds passed, then I said, "I need to know something."

She didn't answer. Just stirred the soup.

"Was Dad involved in the business?"

She faced me. "I spoke to your school counselor this morning about different schools. Grants and assistance. There's a place called Mountain View Prep in Virginia for smart kids that get in trouble. He called them about you and we're eligible."

"Mom—"

She set her mouth. "You need to get back in school."

"What does that have to do with dad? God." I rolled my eyes. "You never let up."

Her chin set and she might as well have spat venom at me. "It has everything to do with your father, and everything else to do with you and what you've been up to. I wasn't born yesterday, Aiden Michael O'Connor, and if I had a mind I'd slap you across the face right now for thinking I'm stupid! You are going to Virginia if it kills me. Do you understand?"

"I'm turning pro, Mom. I am."

"And *I've* decided you are not staying in Boston."

"Mom—"

"I've made my decision, Aiden."

"I'm not leaving."

"You'll do as I say."

I clenched my teeth. "I'm not going anywhere. I'm boxing. And I'm not leaving Angel."

She turned back to the stove. "That's another reason you're going."

"What does that mean?"

"It means she's not right for you."

I clenched my teeth. "So you'd rather have me find a nice Irish Catholic girl so she can end up being a drunk waitress?"

I expected her to come after me. To hit me with the spoon. Throw the pot. Slap me. Something. But she didn't.

With her back to me, silence hammered the kitchen. Her shoulders slumped and she lowered her chin, staring into the soup. Then she sobbed.

"I'm sorry, Mom. I didn't mean that."

Her voice came out weak and soft. "I know how I got my job, Aiden."

"You needed a job."

"At what cost? My son? Who's after you? What did you *do*?" She turned, pausing as she studied my face. "I know Liam, Aiden. You shouldn't be working for him."

"Tell me about Dad."

"He made the same choices you're making right now, and I won't allow you to ruin your life. You're going to Virginia."

"I'm boxing."

She turned, facing me. "I spoke to your counselor about you refusing to go. I'll get a court order if I have to."

"Don't do this, Mom. Please."

She shook her head. "You can hate me, Aiden, but you're going."

I took a breath. "I don't hate you, Mom. But I can't go. Not now."

We stood there across the kitchen from each other, and we both knew something had changed. I realized I wasn't her little boy anymore. She couldn't hit me or spank me or yell at me until I did what she wanted. The last few weeks had proven it.

I was making choices and she couldn't stop me.

So I left, and even as shame burned my cheeks at how I'd treated her, the thought of Angel standing at a stove stirring soup like my mother decided it for me. There would be no Salisbury for my girl.

chapter 32

I glanced at Tommy, who stood leaning against the counter smoking a cigarette. Then I focused back on Liam. "My dad was in jail. I had to bail him out."

Liam smiled, nodding to Tommy. "See, Tommy? That's what I'm talking about. Loyalty. Honor."

Tommy sucked in a lungful of smoke, exhaling. "Whatever. If some drunk spent his life beating the shit out of me, the last thing I'd do is help him. I'd knock him off and piss on his grave."

Liam laughed. "And that's why I have you do what you do, Tommy. Now why don't you run down to the deli and get me a sandwich. Roast beef, light mayo. Ronnie knows how I like it."

Tommy gave me a look so cold I got chills. "Sure," he said.

After Tommy left, Liam lit a cigar. "You should have stayed at Lilly's. You know that, right?"

"Yes."

"These people don't mess around, Aiden."

"I can take care of myself."

He laughed. "You can, but you haven't dealt with these types before."

"You mean because this whole thing isn't just about me punching a kid in the throat?"

He paused, studying me, then nodded. "Who've you been talking to?"

I shrugged.

"Tell me, Aiden."

"I'm not stupid, Liam."

He sat back, crossing his ankle over his knee. "Then go ahead. You tell me."

"What happened with my dad?"

That surprised him, and he took a moment to think about it. "Your father and I grew up together. You know, working. Similar to you and Tommy." He paused.

"Anyway, a few years passed and I found myself in the position to jump ahead, so I did. I had just taken control, and things were shaky." He looked at me. "I'll be blunt, and believe me, I don't like saying this about a kid's father. All those years of me and him working the street together, I knew he took, Aiden. He was a thief, and I overlooked it because we were close. Way-back close. But I couldn't accept it when I became the one he was taking from, so I did him a favor and cut him loose."

"Did him a favor?" I said, not understanding how that would be a favor.

"He's still alive, Aiden. That was my favor."

"So why me? Why'd you pick me?"

"Because I'm still loyal to your father, and also because you've got what it takes. That's why I want you to stop with this boxing bullshit and concentrate on what could take you the furthest." He looked at me. "Nick could have given you and your mother everything I have, Aiden, but he chose a different path. One that hurt you. And it hurts me to see his family suffer for it." He paused. "One day, you'll be sitting in my chair."

I heard what he was saying, but it wasn't connecting. "You still like my dad after he stole from you?"

He nodded. "I loved your father like a brother. We went through some horrible times together, and I'll owe him forever for it. We just can't know each other now. Business is business, and it's best this way."

I thought about it, and realized that the more pieces of this puzzle I put together, the more confused I was. "What's the real story behind Roxbury? I'm not the whole reason for this, am I?"

He studied my face for a few seconds, then answered. "I'm breaking away from the Roxbury people. I have a line on different suppliers; contacts that cut my costs. That also cuts Roxbury out of the chain." He looked at his hands on the table, then back at me. "Even before you crushed that kid's throat, they caught a whiff of things. They're throwing some weight around now, showing me their power. The situation with you just happened to fit their needs."

I grunted. "Lucky me, huh?"

He nodded. "This is a power game, Aiden. Life is a power game, and bottom line is, if you don't have the power, you lose."

"So I'm as good as dead."

"We're all as good as dead, Aiden." He smiled. "It's just the timing that's important."

"So I should just hide?"

He laughed. "You'll do what you need to do, but you have Lilly for protection if you want it. Not much I can say otherwise, is there?"

"No."

"Good. Then keep your eyes open. I'm working on having pressure put on them, but until then, be careful. They've got guys trawling around Southie, making their presence known."

He eyed me, then got up, walking to a cupboard. He opened it and brought back a small pistol, handing it to me. "Use it only if you have to."

I looked at it, felt the weight in my hand, the cool of the metal in my palm. I stuffed it in my pocket. "Okay," I said, uncomfortable with the idea of packing.

I got up, but Liam shook his head and nodded for me to sit back down. I did.

"What?"

"I've got a side deal going. A big one. Big enough to give me the cash I need to break away from Roxbury."

"Oh, yeah?"

"Yeah. It should be an easy transaction, and I want you to be there."

"What's the deal?"

He splayed his hands on the table, staring at the grain in the wood. "Guy contacts me out of the blue, says he has a one-time deal for me. Two point five million street value.

162

I say I'm not interested because it sounds like a setup, but then I check things out with a guy I know who has fingers in with the FBI. Nothing on the radar, so now I'm interested."

"You want me to be there?"

He nodded. "With me, Tommy and Lilly."

"When?"

"Soon. It'll be good for you, Aiden. A step up. I'll cut you in at ten thousand."

I blinked. "Ten thousand?"

"Yes."

"Is that what Tommy's getting?"

He laughed. "Tommy makes a few hundred here and there, buys his mom her dope, wears his clown suits and bling, and he's happy. He'll make his regular cut. So will Lilly."

"Why me?"

"Because I want to show you what we can do. Show you what's possible. You in?"

Ten thousand dollars. Cash.

We could rent a house. I'd have my license soon, and I could buy a car. We could have real furniture. I imagined taking Angel to Abe & Louis, one of the finest restaurants in Boston, and ordering the best on the menu. Maybe steak and lobster. I'd rent a limo to take us. I thought about Razorblade man and his nice condo with the view. I could have that. I could have everything.

I looked at Liam. "Yeah, I'm in."

chapter 33

"Pay attention, Aiden. You've got to concentrate!" Conor held the pads up for me to punch, dodging around the ring and swiping me on the head when I opened up a gap. I'd burnt over two hours in the gym so far, skipping rope for an hour, knocking on the heavy bag, and lifting weights, and now he had me running around the ring trying to catch him.

"If you're going to win the bout next week, you've got to work," he said, swiping me one more time. When I'd arrived at the gym, he was beaming with the news. He'd lined up the fight for next Friday night, and I'd be fighting the guy from New Hampshire he'd talked about.

He found another way in, swapped me, but then he stopped, taking a breath. "What's going on?" he asked.

"What do you mean, 'what's going on'?"

"You're not here, man. You keep looking at that door, like the devil himself is ready to pop through it."

I looked around. "Not here."

He nodded. "Office."

I followed him, biting at my laces as I walked. When we got to the office, he sat behind his desk and said, "Talk."

"Tell me about you and my dad and Liam."

He took a deep breath, looking away. "There's not much to tell."

I withered inside. "Come on, Conor. Don't do this. Tell me. I know my dad was involved with Liam, and that means you were, too. You all go back. What happened?"

"Who's been talking to you?"

I clenched my teeth. "You know who. You've known for a long time. But I don't know if I believe him, and nobody else will tell me."

His eyes met mine, and he nodded. "Okay. We were all involved. Sixteen, seventeen years old, busting beer trucks and garment shipments, selling dope, providing muscle and hustling just about anything we could. Things got more serious as time went by—bigger money, bigger deals. The guy in charge took a liking to Liam. Brought him up as a protégé. Your dad and I were making good money, but Liam was riding high. He was powerful and he used that power well. I was still boxing. Went pro for a little bit, actually. Had three fights. Then I left."

"Why?"

"Because I woke up one night and decided it wasn't for me. I never felt right about it. But I was stuck. I knew I'd never be a great fighter and I had no future. So I disappeared for fifteen years."

"Why'd you come back?"

He smiled, nodding to the door. "Because that old bastard out there, Jim, found me. Told me he was too old to own a gym and that I should have it. I said no for three months, until I realized that I could maybe make a difference around here. Do something for Southie. So I came back."

"What about my dad? Is he a thief? Was he taking?"

He pursed his lips. "I don't know, but there was other trouble between him and Liam."

"Like what?"

He smiled, shaking his head like he was remembering a bad dream. "It was all so typical, Aiden. The oldest story in the book. Liam had a thing for your mother. She chose your father. He didn't like it, so he used his power against your father."

"If he hated my dad, why'd he take me in, then? It makes no sense."

Conor shrugged. "Only he knows that, Aiden, but Liam is a strange mix. He cares in his own way about the people here, and he's fiercely loyal. He leaves my business alone for that reason, and he's left your father alone for those same reasons."

I frowned. "It makes no sense, though."

Conor looked at me. "Have you ever hated somebody you love, Aiden?"

I thought of my dad. And my mom. "Yeah."

He shrugged. "Your father, Liam and I were like brothers, and even if I hate my brother, I still love him, and I can't make it go away. Liam might have a lot of hate in him and he'll crush anyone he sees as a threat, but there's also love. I think he was hurt when your mother chose Nick, but

I also think he can't erase what your father meant to him all those years ago." He shook his head, then went on. "He can be the most understanding person you'd ever meet, but also the most unforgiving, merciless bastard on the planet."

I slumped in my chair and groaned. "This sucks."

He leveled a stare at me. "People are after you, huh?"

I nodded, explaining some of the situation to him.

He listened, then took a gulp of coffee. The clock on the wall ticked, and then he said, "I can't tell you what to do, Aiden. But I know how you feel. We all do, because we were *all* you at that age—poor, angry, frustrated and hopeless. Some of us still are. But I don't think you want what Liam has to offer. The price is too high."

"Maybe."

"You can box, Aiden. You can succeed." He picked up a pen, fiddling with it for a moment. "I think your mom's right—you should go to Virginia."

"She talked to you, didn't she?"

"Yes."

"I'm not leaving."

"You can come back and box, Aiden. You're young. Just get out of here for awhile. Graduate."

"I'm not running away. Not like some coward."

He blinked and I knew I'd hurt him. I was getting so good at hurting people, it made me sick. He swallowed. "I did run. I abandoned everybody. But I don't regret it, because if I had stayed, I wouldn't be sitting here right now, talking to you." He looked away. "I'd probably be dead, or sitting in the back room of that pub, telling you who to kill."

"I'm not killing anybody."

"You will. You can't get to where you want without it."

I looked at him. "Your story is bullshit. You didn't choose to leave, did you? You killed somebody."

A long silence followed. I felt my breathing and heard his, and with it the echoes of the gym faded. The goddamned clock kept ticking, and then he nodded.

"What happened?"

"It doesn't matter what happened. Only that I ran from it, and now I live with it."

"You did it for Liam, didn't you? That's why he's left you alone since you came back." I looked at him. "Liam owes you, doesn't he?"

He cut in. "Think about what you want, Aiden. But remember, only you can make the decisions."

chapter 34

I walked around Southie for four hours after leaving the gym, wondering how the truth could be so complicated. I wanted it in black and white. Easy to figure out. But it wasn't. I could hurt people with the truth, and the truth could hurt me. But I could also ease somebody else's pain with that same truth—I could use it any way I wanted. It made me realize that the truth was only the truth if you saw it that way. There *was* no black and white, and Mr. Langdon was right. I was starting to get it—the Golden Rule. It wasn't about *not* hurting people; it was more like who'd be hurt the least.

"Kill 'em all and let God sort 'em out." I'd heard that saying as far back as I could remember, and I understood it now. Only God knew. He was the only one with the right answers, and in this world, it was eat or be eaten, kill or be killed. Never trust anybody, because if you did, they'd end up taking what was yours.

Liam knew what he was talking about, and I grunted at the irony of Liam and Mr. Langdon. They'd both said the same things, only in different ways.

But my immediate problem, and the main reason I'd been walking for so long, was that I had no place to stay. I wasn't about to put my mom in danger by going home. The thought of staying with Lilly and putting up with his fat mouth was out of the question, and Tommy just wasn't Tommy anymore.

He'd found the dollar and the power, and every time I saw him, I saw it in his eyes. I was now a challenge to him. A threat. If some guy'd come up to me a year ago and told me I wouldn't trust my best friend in a year, I'd have laughed in his face. We'd always been tight—as tight as brothers. Not anymore.

So I kept walking. I ended up across the street from Angel's, staring up at her windows. The pawn shop's fluorescent sign glowed on the sidewalk and I wondered what she was doing. Sleeping. Reading. Maybe studying. I wanted to be with her so much. And I wanted to be something *to* her, *for* her.

Then I saw it: a FOR SALE sign in the pawn shop window. Angel had told me her father was sick and that things weren't going well. But I didn't realize how bad it was; a shiver went up my spine as I thought about her. He'd be dead soon. The old guy probably didn't have a dime to his name, and that meant Angel would be in trouble. Maybe she'd even be shipped back to Cuba to be with her relatives—away from here, away from me.

But it didn't have to be that way. I'd have ten thousand in cash soon, and I knew there'd be more coming in after that. I could find us an apartment, Angel and me; a nice one.

She wouldn't have to worry. She wouldn't need to go away, and I'd give her everything she wanted.

Conor was wrong. The price wasn't too high. I was making the choices that would hurt the least.

◆

I left Angel's street and made my way to the pub. The couch there would be better than anywhere else I could think of, and sleep was creeping under my eyelids as I walked. All this thinking was wearing me out and more tiring than working the bag for two hours. My mind was done.

As I rounded the corner and headed up the hill to the pub, my feet dragging and my eyes bleary, I suddenly stopped. Just past the pub at the curb sat a silver Chevy Tahoe, plumes of exhaust steaming from the tailpipes.

I stepped back into the shadows and away from the street lights, knowing I should book it to the beach or the park; go anywhere but here. Liam's warning came back to me: Pressure. Domination. It didn't matter what I was to them or to Liam. I was being used as a chess piece, just a pawn in a bigger game on a board that I couldn't even see. I was nothing more than a payment, a sacrifice to set up a victory.

"I wouldn't go up there if I were you."

I jumped, every hair on my body prickling as I spun around. A man stood farther back in the shadows. As my eyes adjusted and I slipped my hand to my pocket, feeling for the pistol Liam had given me, the shadow spoke again, his voice calm and easy.

"You won't need that, Aiden."

I squinted, trying to make the guy out. "Who are you?"

"You don't know me."

I wrapped my fingers around the handle of the pistol.

"Step farther back in the shadows. They might see you."

I kept my eyes on the figure, stepping to the side as I slid the pistol from my pocket. He backed up a step. I swallowed and said, "Talk."

"My name is John Kirkland, and I think I might be able to help you."

"With what?"

"With that truck up there. Maybe with more."

"Who are you with?"

"Nobody."

"Bullshit."

He didn't respond.

This guy didn't talk Southie, didn't sound like that slime ball from Roxbury I'd met in the back of the pub, and the way he spoke reminded me of my English teacher. Guys with college degrees talked different.

"You a cop?" I asked.

"I work for the Federal Bureau of Investigation."

I almost bolted.

"I can make things easier for you, Aiden."

"I haven't done anything."

"That man up the street thinks you have."

"I don't know what you're talking about."

"You're in a lot of trouble."

"What do you want?"

"I can make your problems go away. Get you out of this."

"I'm not a snitch."

"We're not interested in Liam. We just want to maintain contact with you. That's all."

"I'm not stupid."

"I know. But you're a kid, and I don't want to see you end up like your buddy, Ben Capo."

I thought back to that first shakedown Tommy and I did for Liam. Ben Capo died because of it.

"He wasn't my buddy," I told the FBI agent.

"Do you know what it means, being an accomplice to murder, Aiden?"

I didn't say a word.

"You and Tommy McAllister shook him down, and the next thing we know, Mr. Capo is dead, with a plastic bag over his head."

"He owed other people money."

"We have surveillance tapes of you visiting Mr. Capo. The next time we see him, he's a corpse."

"Prove who you are, then."

His tone softened. "I'm not here to threaten you, Aiden. Ben Capo was a nothing, and honestly, we're after something else."

"I don't know anything."

He reached into his jacket pocket slowly and I saw a flash of white in the shadows. "Here," he said. "Take this. If you get into a jam, give me a call." He held out a business card.

I looked at it, then glanced over my shoulder toward

the Tahoe still idling at the curb. I took it, sliding it into my back pocket. "Sure."

"You need a place to stay tonight?"

I shook my head.

"I can help you with that, too."

I tucked the pistol back in my pocket. "I'm fine."

A funny lilt came to his voice. "Suit yourself, then."

"Yeah, I will."

Then he was gone, melting into the shadows.

◆

I stood there for a long time, my eyes wandering up the street to the still-running Tahoe, my thoughts flickering to the card in my back pocket. It was a three-sided chess game now. I was being used by three sides to each get what they wanted. The only difference was that Liam was paying me for it, big time.

But a wad of money in my pocket wouldn't make much of a difference if I was dead, which was probably what the guy in that Tahoe was planning for me.

I backtracked, skirting through an alley and around the block, coming back to the street farther away from the Tahoe. A horn honked in the distance, echoing through the streets, and I jumped when a mangy dog scurried from under a stack of cardboard boxes piled at the entrance to another alley.

Then, out of nowhere, a hand yanked me back and into the darkness.

I struggled, fighting to get the pistol from my pocket,

but a huge forearm locked itself around my neck, tightening like a python squeezing its prey. A second later, the guy pounded his fist into my kidney and I doubled over. At the same time, he jerked me upright by the neck, tightening and choking me as he landed another kidney punch.

The next thing I knew, I was thrown to the ground as stars danced before my eyes. I felt for the pistol but it was gone, and a feeling of dread seared through me.

There in the dark alley, I focused my eyes on the figure standing upright now, his shadow blending into the wall behind him. I squinted, recognizing him, my chest still heaving.

"Lilly?" I said.

"Shut the fuck up, kid."

I winced as I got to my feet. "What's going on?" I said, and then I saw it. He was holding a pistol and it was pointed at me. "Whoa," I told him. "Hold on, man. I'm not the bad guy here."

"We'll see about that."

Then it clicked in my head. "You saw me talking to that guy?"

His voice came low and menacing. "Yes."

Panic swept through me. "It's not what you think. I've never seen the guy before. But he knows, man. They've got surveillance."

"And I should believe a punk snitch who's two-bit loser father took from the organization?"

"I'm not a snitch and you know it."

"How would I know?"

"Because you saw it, you fucking idiot. He came at me

from behind, in the shadows. They've been following the guys in the Tahoe. And you—all of us."

I reached in my back pocket, taking out the card. "Here's his card, too. You think if I was working with them I'd have this on me?"

"He tried to bring you in, then? Get you to talk?"

I nodded. "Yeah. Threatened me with Capo's murder, too. Me and Tommy." I looked toward the street. "That means they're on Tommy, too."

"What'd he say?"

"That he could help me."

"With what?"

I pointed down the street toward the Tahoe. "The guys that are after me, Capo, all of it."

"You know Liam's going to hear about this," Lilly said.

"He'll hear about it because I'm going to be the one telling him," I said. "I'm not a snitch, Lilly. That guy told me they weren't even interested in Liam. They're after bigger stuff."

I shook my head. "Besides, for all I know, you're the one talking."

He laughed. "Yeah, sure."

"Then what are you doing here, huh?" I asked.

"I'm taking care of business."

"What business?"

He peeked around the edge of the building, spying the Tahoe with the guy sitting in it. "*That* business," he told me. "Come on."

I followed Lilly out of the alley, tracing his steps and

staying close to the walls of the buildings we passed, my heart pounding the whole time. *Business* to Liam was different from *business* to Lilly, and I was nervous.

Liam handled business with money and words. Lilly didn't say a word when he conducted his business, and as we snuck up to the rear of the Tahoe, I wasn't so sure I wanted to have any part of what he was about to do.

Too late to turn back, I watched as Lilly straightened up and strode up to the truck's door. He smashed his elbow through the window, reached in with both hands, grabbing the man's hair. Then he yanked, pulling with the full force of his body, and dragged the guy *through* the window, dumping him onto the street.

Flailing and fighting the entire way as Lilly dragged him across the street and into the alley, the man was eerily silent like the clips of old movies on TV. In the darkness, I followed them down the narrow, trash-strewn path until Lilly came to a door. Still holding the guy by the hair, Lilly kicked open the door and jerked the guy inside.

I followed, my body twitching, every hair on end. It was an abandoned warehouse, and with the moon shining through the upper windows, I could see the broken storage shelves, wooden pallets and assorted junk strewn all around. The place smelled like old clothes; musty, forgotten and unused. I stifled a cough, and Lilly threw a well-aimed left into the man's face, then told me to find a rope.

I stood frozen, watching blood, black in the moonlight, drip from the man's mouth.

"Goddamn it, kid, over there. On that shelf. The rope. Go get it!" Lilly said as the man struggled.

I turned, hearing Lilly land another punch, and grabbed the rope, turning back and throwing it to Lilly.

"You think this is some stinking movie, kid? Come here and tie him up."

I gritted my teeth, picked up the rope and secured the guy's wrists behind his back. Lilly still kept hold of the guy's hair and I turned to look at the guy as I moved away. He was well built, but no match for Lilly's size and brute strength. His breath was raspy now, and his mouth contorted with pain and fear. Now that I had a closer look, I recognized him as one of the men who'd chased Angel and me that night in the park.

Lilly yanked him to his knees, then released him, stepping back. Silence—except for the guy's breathing—filled the empty space.

Lilly leaned against a metal desk, rubbing the elbow that he'd used to break the car window. He smiled in the opaque moonlight. "Well, here we all are."

The man slumped on his knees, reminding me of the pictures I'd seen on the news of the prisoners in the Middle East. But this wasn't a war zone; it was Southie, and not ten minutes before, I'd been talking to an FBI agent. I shook my head.

"The FBI has surveillance, Lil. Come on. They probably watched the whole thing."

He laughed, his low voice echoing. "Get smart, kid."

"What?"

"It was a setup. Liam needed to know if you'd cave."

I studied his face. "He wasn't FBI?"

"Hell yes, he's FBI, but he flipped. On the payroll, you

could say." He kept his eyes on the man. "You hear me! We have 'em in our pocket, and you want to come here and start trouble?"

He walked over, grabbing the man's hair once again and jerking his chin up. "You want to come here and tell us who's in charge? That it? You think you can come here and run us?"

He glanced at me. "Roxbury greasers think they have our nuts tied in a knot, kid, but things just changed." He shook his head. "Ain't gonna' happen, dog. Ain't gonna' happen, and I'm going to send you back as a present to show them."

With that, Lilly looked at me and the gleam in his eyes lit against the moonlight. He was like a little boy about to stick his hand in the candy jar. He reached into his pocket, taking out a plastic bag. I stepped back and he let out a short laugh. "No worries, kid," he said. "This ain't your time. Coming soon enough, but not tonight. Go on, get out."

"Lilly…"

With his hand still clenching the guy's hair, Lilly shook out the bag. The man struggled, and Lilly, bag in hand, curled a thick fist, jacking the guy in the face again. He stilled. Then Lilly opened the bag with his teeth, readying it, looked at me again and shrugged. "You want to watch, then? My pleasure. Your *buddy* likes watching."

I shook my head, wide eyed and sick to my stomach. Then I left.

chapter 35

"Three rounds, Aiden. You can wear him out if you go the distance. I know you can." Conor said as he checked my gloves.

The moment had come: my first pro fight. A week had passed since that night in the warehouse. I'd come to think of it as "Lilly's Nightmare." I hadn't heard a word about it from anybody. I'd looked in the newspapers, nothing. Watched the news on TV—not a thing. I was learning that when invisible people disappeared, nobody missed them. I was becoming invisible, too, and I didn't like the feeling at all.

Liam had laughed hysterically when he explained about the FBI agent who'd tested me. He'd clapped me on the back, offered me a shot of Irish whiskey—which I took—and then congratulated me.

"Life is always a test," he'd said. Every day you had to prove who you were and what you stood for in this world, and he was proud of me. He said he'd also set me up to show me how powerful he was, and, how powerful *I* could be. Then he'd handed me an envelope with a thousand dollars in it. Tommy glared at me the whole time.

Since then I'd trained at the gym. I'd worked my body to the bone to keep my mind from that look in Lilly's eyes when he'd taken the bag out of his pocket. I'd punched the heavy bag until my knuckles hurt enough to wipe the image of that night from my mind, but it always came back. I realized then that Lilly'd killed Ben Capo, too, and that he'd enjoyed it.

There was no other time in my life when things were so split in half. There was this life—my boxing life—and my other life, the one where I worked for Liam. That was the life where words weren't spoken and men were killed, and where power and money were all that mattered. That was the life where I could be something, the life that could mean I'd never see another Salisbury steak.

I hadn't seen my mom for over a week because she'd promised to send me away. I'd deposited money in her account to help her pay the bills, but I knew that nothing had changed. I wasn't going anywhere, and she'd try and make me.

The Roxbury people were gone for now, and Angel and I spent as much time together as possible. Her father was wasting away, barely able to work more than a few hours at a time.

But I still had this—my time in the ring. I couldn't let go of it, no matter what Liam said, or how often he told me I was a fool for boxing like a street punk with nothing better to look forward to than a bruised brain and cauliflower ears.

Conor saw something in me that made me believe, and, as I sat on my stool in the corner of the ring looking at my opponent, I realized how much I loved it. Not just hitting people—that wasn't it. I loved it because I was good at it, and I loved it because I could win.

The purse was four hundred and thirty-five dollars that night. Minus the entrance fee, I'd make a little less than a quarter of what I'd make in one night of working for Liam. And that was only if I won.

In that sense, Liam was right. Even if I won every fight, I couldn't live on two or three fights a month. I'd be training during the day and working a graveyard shift somewhere, emptying garbage cans to make rent, and I'd do it until I either made it big or wore my body out and ended up with nothing.

One of the things Liam always talked about was knowing where you were now so you could read the future. I knew where I was now. I was on a battlefield, and if I lost this fight, Liam would win. I'd be stuck in that life forever.

"Watch his right, Aiden," Conor told me. "He's a precision fighter, not a brawler, and he'll hit your sweet spot if he gets the chance."

I glanced around the gym, nodding distractedly as I watched my mother walk through the doors. I sighed and said to Conor, "You told her, didn't you?"

"She's your mother."

"Why? You know she'll probably have the cops here to take me away and send me to Virginia."

"No, she won't. I made a deal with her. She needs to see you win, Aiden. See how good you are. She promised."

I swallowed as the announcer made his way to center ring and began speaking to the crowd.

"Shit," I said, rattled from seeing my mother there in the one place that was truly mine.

"Make her proud, Aiden. Show her what you can do."

◆

By the second round, I decided that my body was nothing more than a landing site for precision-guided missiles launched by a guy named Giovanni Maniro from East Boston. I was being schooled by him, and even though we went punch for punch, my shots lacked the kind of power he packed. My mother sat in the stands with her hand over her mouth, and I was crumbling. Tired and winded. My opponent was merciless on my midsection, only throwing face shots to distract me and get an opening to the ribs. Mostly I was playing catch-up.

I'd landed four or five solid rights to his jaw, and at least one time I managed to stun him. But I'd been too winded to follow through and finish the job. He danced back, closed up, and then clinched with me when I tried to open up on him. He was good; he knew me and knew the way I fought.

I had to do something to change things, and do it now. Liam had told me that only the stupid kept doing the same thing over and over, failing time and again. And Conor taught me that sticking to your training was the only way to win. But this guy, toe to toe and punch for punch, was better trained than I was. And every time I made a mistake, he capitalized on it.

I tasted blood through my mouthpiece, and the golf-ball sized contusion above my eye was stretching the skin on my eyebrow, making it tight and throbbing, exploding in pain every time the bastard zeroed in on it. He delivered five or six shots to my midsection, followed by what felt like a bullet to my head.

I knew he was tired because I'd pounded him right back; but he was also wearing out because he hit so damned hard. Even so, my war of attrition against him wasn't working. I couldn't outlast him, and if the bell rang after the third round, they'd hold up his hand. He'd be the point winner. No TKO, but a win nonetheless—unless my head wasn't where it was supposed to be; unless my body wasn't, either.

Giovanni controlled the center of the ring, moving me clockwise around the ropes. I barreled straight into him, spun him in the clinch, then threw him back, changing my stance to southpaw.

I could hit left-handed but not so effectively, and when he came in and tried to take center ring back, I lit him up with a flurry of hits, surprising him with a big uppercut from the left that had him staggering backward. Conor screamed for me to move to him, and Giovanni's corner was screaming to take up a guarded position against a left-handed boxer, but I didn't listen. I wanted him to come in to me, ready for the left.

He did, and as he moved in I danced forward, pivoting

my hips, changing stances and driving in with the hardest right-hand roundhouse I could muster. Bull's-eye! I felt the force up my arm and into my shoulder, that electric jolt telling me I'd hurt him—and I had.

He went down to a knee and the ref jumped between us, shoving me back. Facing Giovanni, the ref called for a ten-count.

As the seconds slid by, I turned, glancing at Conor; he was studying me, his expression perplexed. I smiled, tapping my head. He smiled back, shaking his. Ten seconds later, the ref called it.

I'd won. I really won!

Then someone said, "Liam wants to see you."

Tommy looked up at me as Conor slapped an ice ring on my eye. The crowd was dispersing, and as I sat on the stool, I smiled.

"You see it, Tommy? I won. First pro fight, and I won."

"Yeah, sure. Great. Did you hear me?"

"Yeah. I'll go later."

He shook his head. "He said *now*."

Conor swiveled his head. "He'll be there when he's there."

Tommy looked at me. "So this is your trainer guy, huh?"

Conor leaned over the ropes, closer to Tommy. "Yeah, I am. And I don't like your kind in my gym. Get out."

Tommy's eyes flashed. "You'd better watch your mouth."

"Only thing I'll watch is your ass leaving this building. I said, get out."

I cut in. "Whoa, it's cool. This is Tommy, my old buddy. You know."

Conor's eyes were steady on Tommy. "Yeah, I know. Now get out."

Tommy backed away, murder in his eyes. "Sure, man. I'll leave. But you'll be hearing about this, huh?"

Conor laughed. "Don't threaten me, punk."

Tommy laughed back and then he was gone, melting into the remaining crowd.

I untied my other glove. "Damn, Conor, what was that all about?"

"Liam and I have a deal."

"What deal?"

"He keeps his business out of my gym."

My mind flashed to the story he'd told me about why he'd left Southie.

"Tommy probably doesn't know that."

"He does now."

"Why the anger, Conor?"

He looked at me. "Because I know this game, Aiden." He pulled my glove off. "Get showered. We have someplace to go."

I furrowed my brow. "Where?"

He pointed toward the door. "You heard your friend. We have an appointment with Liam."

chapter 36

My mind swam as I showered. I was almost in a frenzy about Conor coming with me to see Liam, and as I dragged my street clothes on and met him outside, I was jittery. And my mom had left without saying a word.

Conor took his keys from his pocket. "Come on. I'll give you a lift."

So we drove, and we didn't talk the whole way.

When we arrived at the bar, Lilly stood outside having a cigarette. He smiled at Conor, "Hey, old man. Good to see you."

Conor shot him a scowl. "Cut it with the shit, Lil. I'm here on business and you know why."

Lilly smiled and held up his palms. "Hey, hey now, Conor. We go back, right? I do my job, you do yours, huh?"

Conor turned away and walked toward the door.

Lilly crushed his smoke under his heel. "No can do, Chief. Liam wants to see the kid. *Alone*."

Conor bristled, his huge neck muscles bulging as he faced Lilly. They stood so close, their noses almost touched.

"You going to stop me, Lilly?" Conor growled.

Lilly grinned. " 'Course I ain't, Conor. Just following orders."

"Good. Go get an ice cream, then." Conor told him, then walked inside.

I followed. Tommy sat on a bar stool at the back counter, and Liam was sitting at the table talking to a guy named Ike Curley, who I'd seen around a few times. Liam looked up at Conor, nodded and told Ike to leave, which he did.

Liam splayed his hands on the table, leaning back in his chair. "Been a long time since you were in this room, Conor."

"Looks like we have a problem, Liam," he said.

Liam nodded.

Conor pointed at Tommy. "Keep your dogs away from my gym."

Tommy cut in. "I ain't a dog, you prick."

Conor went on. "Get him out of here before I wash his mouth out with my fist, Liam."

"He's fine where he is, Conor."

Conor's jaw muscles worked. "Then control him."

Liam smiled. "I can promise you that Tommy will not say another word," he said, glancing at Tommy. "Now, back to our problem."

"I know what this is about and I don't appreciate it," Conor told him.

"Our deal was that I stay out of your world and you stay out of mine, Conor." Liam nodded to me. "That's part of my world, and I was just reminding you of that."

Conor shook his head. "Leave him be."

"You know how much I respect you, Conor. All those years ago. The prison time. You never snitched. And I gave you my word. But you can't come in here and tell me what is my business and what isn't."

I blinked. *Prison?*

Liam noticed and smiled. "You didn't know, Aiden?" He looked at Conor. "Why don't you tell him, Conor? Tell him that you took the fall for offing that fucker, spent ten years inside, and when you came back, I gave you eighty grand free and clear to buy the gym—because you're an honorable man, and because I loved you like my own blood. Then we made our deal; I respect your decision to get out of the business, you respect my business."

I looked at Conor. "Is that true? Prison?"

He nodded. "I told you I left. It was none of your business," He glared at Liam. "Or anybody else's business, where I was." He went on, his voice lowering and his eyes darkening. "And none of that changes the fact that this kid isn't yours. Never was, never will be. You got it?"

"And you say this to me?" Liam smiled. "Who are *you*? His father?"

"Don't start with me, Liam. Aiden chose to box and you slapped me in the face by sending that punk to my gym," Conor warned.

Liam sat back, his face straight, his eyes piercing. "Why do you care so much about this kid? Almost like," he said, glancing at me, "you're more than just his trainer." He paused, then went on. "By the way, how is Aiden's mother? I hear you've been spending quite a bit of time with her lately."

189

My jaw dropped. I looked at Conor. "You—you've been—"

Conor looked at me, taking a breath. "We're concerned about you, Aiden. That's all."

I clenched my teeth.

"Aiden—" Conor began.

Liam cut in. "Why don't we let *him* decide. Fair is fair." He looked at me. "Make your decision, Aiden. End this conflict."

Conor began. "Bullshit. He's a boy, not a man, Liam. And now is not the time to press it."

I cut in, staring at Conor. "Are you banging my *mother*?"

Conor winced. "Aiden, your mom and I have been talking quite a bit about you lately, and we've gone to dinner a few times. That's all."

I had no words. I couldn't believe it.

"Decision time, Aiden," Liam said, smiling. "And I give both of you my word that whatever Aiden decides, I will respect it. End of story."

Conor shook his head. "No deal, Liam. This isn't right and you know it."

I looked at Conor, our eyes meeting. My jaw hurt from clenching my teeth so hard.

"Stay away from my mother," I told him.

"Aiden, please. Can't you see what he's doing? He's twisting things. He—"

So many lies, I thought. Everybody was a liar. I shook my head, interrupting him. "You bastard."

Liam stood. "I think we have our answer, Conor."

Conor's eyes didn't leave mine. "This is it, then?"

A long moment passed with our eyes locked. How could he? He'd led me on and pretended to give a crap, and it was all just to screw my mother.

"Fuck you, Conor. I said stay away from her. My father might be a drunk and a jerk, but they're still married," I said.

There was total silence in the room, and after a moment, Conor turned and left.

When the door slammed shut, Liam and I didn't speak for several minutes. Then he walked to the counter, poured himself a shot of whiskey, downed it and handed me one, saying, "You okay?"

I swallowed the booze, feeling the instant burn. My chest relaxed and my head got light. "Yeah," I said. "I'm fine."

He smiled, clapping me on the shoulder. "Good. Then let's get down to business. We've got some planning to do for the deal coming up."

"That's still on?"

"Yes. The Roxbury people will be compensated and I'm ironing things out as we speak."

"Lilly killed—"

He shook his head. "We don't speak of some things, Aiden. Lilly has been instrumental in letting our business partners know where we stand, and we'll still be doing business with them—just under different terms."

Reading between the lines, I figured an uneasy compromise had been reached to stop an all-out war from happening. "And the Cuban guy?"

"A tremendous opportunity for us. And for you. In fact,

I've decided to up your stake. Fifteen thousand will be your cut." He smiled. You'll be my number two on this one."

"Fifteen thousand?"

He nodded. "In fact…" He picked up an envelope from the table. "Here's seventy-five hundred of it right now. Good faith on my part." He held out the money to me.

I looked at it. I could do anything with that. Buy a car. Get an apartment. New clothes.

I took it. "Deal."

Liam nodded. "That's my boy. Now, sit down and we'll hammer this out."

chapter 37

Angel sat across the table from me, looking just like her name. In the dim light of the restaurant, with the candle flickering between us, she was every dream I'd ever had about my life. With a thousand dollars cash in my pocket, I'd rented a limo, picked her up after work at the pawn shop, and we'd gone shopping. I bought her a new dress, shoes, a necklace and a purse, and she picked out a Tommy Hilfiger suit for me. Then, with Liam's help in the form of a quick phone call, we scored a table at Dabios, the best restaurant in Boston.

Her eyes danced in the candlelight, excitement coursing through both of us. Like me, she'd never ridden in a limo, and when we first opened up the menus and saw the prices, her eyes widened. "Oh, my god," she'd said. "This place is expensive."

I'd laughed, ordering huge shrimp cocktails, then trying in vain to get us a bottle of wine. She looked older than I did, the finest of fine ladies in her dress and with her makeup done. But I didn't and couldn't convince the waiter that I was old enough to drink legally. We both laughed when the waiter smiled and shook his head, then we ordered Cokes instead.

I looked around the restaurant as we sat and talked. This was me. This place was where I belonged. I ate it up with my eyes. I'd arrived and I wasn't going anywhere anytime soon. As our second appetizer arrived, I leaned forward and took her hand in mine with a grin.

"There might be some beautiful women in here tonight, but you put them all to shame."

She laughed, throaty and sincere, and told me I was a bad boy. "Don't be rude, Aiden."

I smiled. "The truth is never rude. You're beautiful."

She looked down at the saucer with the cocktail sauce on it. "You won this much money from the fight today?"

I touched the goose egg on my eyebrow. The swelling had gone down a bit. "Four hundred and sixty-five dollars."

She kept her chin down. "This night is costing way more than that."

"I've been saving up."

"Aiden…"

I wrapped my other hand around hers. "I'm going to take care of you. Get you an apartment when you need it."

Her chin quivered.

"I'm sorry. I shouldn't have brought it up," I told her.

"He'll be gone soon," she said.

"I know. But you don't have to worry about anything but him. Let me take care of everything else."

"I can't let you do that, Aiden."

"Why not?"

"Because."

I took a breath. "I love you, Angel. I want you to marry me, and I don't care what anybody says, either."

"We're too young."

"So then we'll wait."

"But what if things don't work out? I can't let you do all this stuff. You'd end up hating me."

"Do you love me?"

She sniffed, squeezing my hand. "Yes. I think so."

I nodded. "Then that's enough for me. We can take the rest as it goes. And besides, I could never hate you."

She wiped her nose with her napkin, placing it gently on her lap. "I'm sorry. I'm ruining this amazing night."

I laughed. "You couldn't ruin anything." I paused. "Let's make a deal?"

"What kind of deal?"

"We live tonight for tonight and forget about everything else. Let it just be about you and me and this fantastic place."

She sniffed again, giggled, and then looked into my eyes and said, "That's why I like you."

"Why? Because I look so hot in this suit that you can't wait to get your hands on me?"

She laughed. "Well, that, and you have a way of just taking me out of a bad place when I'm down, and making me forget all the other crap in my life."

"I know. I'm brilliant, huh?"

She took a sip of her Coke, looking at me over the rim of her glass. "I remember when we first met."

"Yeah?"

"Yeah. You couldn't even say a sentence without goofing up."

I shrugged. "I was nervous."

"You? Nervous? Mr. Don Juan, sitting here in his fine clothes, eating shrimp big enough to put a leash on?"

"If I can get my head beat in a ring, I can handle a fancy restaurant."

She looked around. "I sort of feel like a fish out of water here."

"Ha. Me, too. But it's nice, huh?"

"I could get used to it."

"Good, because it'll happen again. And that steak I ordered is going to disappear five minutes after they put it in front of me."

She laughed. "I'm savoring mine. Anything that costs forty bucks is worth taking your time over."

I held up my glass in a toast. "Then I will, too." We clinked our glasses together. "Here's to never eating Salisbury steak again. Ever."

She furrowed her brow.

"Inside joke. Sorry. It's like fake steak and it's awful."

She laughed, and then our steaks arrived. We ate—slowly. And it took every ounce of willpower for me not to pick it up and stuff the whole thing into my mouth. It was the best steak I'd ever had.

After a dessert called crème brulee, which I'd never heard of but that Angel insisted on, we sat for awhile longer, talking about Southie and my history here. We talked about her family in Cuba, too, and I found out that we weren't all that different. Family and religion and roots meant just as much to Irish Catholics as they did to Cubans, and both of our backgrounds were stories of the same type of poor, struggling, hardworking people.

When we were leaving and I opened the restaurant door for her, then saw the limo waiting for us, I couldn't help but smile. If I'd told myself a year ago that I'd be walking out of the finest joint in Boston with a girl like Angel, then riding home in a limo, I'd have laughed at myself for being such a dreamer and fool.

But here I was, and I never wanted the night to end.

Back in the limo, I turned the radio on low and we toasted cold cans of Coke. "To the high life," she said, laughing until she had to hold her stomach.

"I have a surprise for you," I said, as the city lights streamed by.

"Oh?"

"Yes."

She squeezed my hand. "Sounds mysterious."

"It'll be up to you."

She cleared her throat. "Hmmm. What is it?"

"I got a room at the Hilton. Actually, a suite. For us." I hesitated, feeling instant tension from her. "But only if you want to go."

She was silent and her hand went slack in mine.

I shook my head. "It's okay. Really. Not a problem."

"No, Aiden, it's not that. Not because it's you, I mean. We haven't been together long, and I don't think I'm ready for that."

"I understand. No pressure." I smiled. "I haven't even really felt you up yet, anyway. You know?"

She looked down and I saw a trace of a smile on her face.

I laughed, trying to put her at ease.

"I embarrassed you, huh?" I said.

She glanced at me, then looked down. "Have you ever...uh, you know...?"

"Nope." I snuck a look at her and a drip of sweat ran down my back. "Have you?" I asked.

She looked away.

"Sorry. None of my business."

"Only once. It was a mistake."

Dreaded silence followed, so I put my arm around her, leaned in close and kissed her. "That's okay. There's always tomorrow. Or the next day. Or next year," I whispered.

She giggled, loosening up, then kissed me back. "It's really a suite?"

I nodded. "Top floor, with a balcony overlooking the city. And a Jacuzzi. They said they have TVs and phones in the bathrooms, even."

Her eyes widened. "Wow."

"How about we go check it out. No funny business, either. Just see how the high rollers live."

She smiled, snuggling up against me. "I suppose a little bit of funny business might be okay."

I almost jumped out of my skin, then took a breath. "Well, I don't know. I'm not really that kind of a guy."

She slapped my arm, moving away. "Jerk."

I slid across the seat to her and kissed her again. "Okay, fine. A *little* funny business." Then I kissed her all the way to the hotel.

We spent the night together in that suite at the Hilton, standing on the balcony overlooking the city until the sun came up.

chapter 38

Angel would catch hell from her father for being out all night, and after I called a taxi for her, I lay back on the hotel bed and stared at the ceiling.

Everything was clear now. My mom. Conor. Boxing. There was always an agenda.

Conor bullshitting me about how much he wanted to see me go pro. Filling my head with dreams about being anything other than a low-rank Southie pro, scratching to make a living while I got my brains beat out in the ring. All that just so he could get close to my mom.

And my mom wasn't much better. She was married, for one. She was willing to send me to some private school for "troubled teens" to get rid of me, huh? Send me away so she could be with her new boyfriend. So who really was the troubled one?

I'd cleaned up her puke, carried her to bed, saw her piss herself because she was so drunk, and now she was dating my trainer—who just happened to be one of my dad's old school buddies. It was too much.

My life was a fucked-up Jerry Springer episode and I was so pissed off I could spit bullets.

If I'd had my way, Aiden O'Connor wouldn't be an O'Connor. I'd slide out of my skin and walk out of this hotel as somebody else—a whole different person. I wanted to be a stranger to the parents who were supposed to be mine. I pictured myself ordering a beer from my mom at the bar, looking into her eyes, and her not ever knowing me.

I'd see my low-life father in the gutter one night, drunk out of his mind, slobbering, dirty, stained and angry. I'd walk right on by, sure not to get his filth on my shoes. Maybe they deserved the lives that they'd made, but I didn't think I deserved the life they'd stuck me with.

They made me who I was. My dad beat it into me with his fists, and my mom put up with it from him; and then she watched him do it to me.

I fumed, remembering the day I'd introduced her to Angel. That look of disapproval in her eyes. She'd never made over nine bucks an hour, lived in the projects, drank until she blacked out—and yet there she stood, judging Angel because of her skin color and her religion? Angel wasn't good enough for her? What a joke.

If there was one thing my parents would find out soon enough, it was that I wasn't anything like them. I'd be more, I'd be better, and I'd do it the way I wanted. And I didn't need them or anybody else pretending to help me, or pretending to care.

I took a cab home, still in the suit from the night before. People stared at me when I handed the cabbie a twenty, then went up the stairs and down the hall. I slid my key into the lock and opened the door; the apartment was silent, the musty smell familiar.

Looking at the kitchen table, I grimaced. Two dirty plates sat on the counter next to the sink, along with two glasses. I clenched my teeth.

I went through the living room and down the short hall. My room was empty and my bed still unmade from the previous morning when I'd gone out.

The door to my mother's room was closed and I opened it.

Conor was just buckling his belt, shirtless and barefoot. Mom was still under the covers, leaning on her elbow, the sleep still in her eyes. Conor straightened up and our eyes met.

I flew at him, tackling him on the bed and straddling him, my mom scrambling to the side as I threw punch after punch at his face. I was on top of him, jack-hammering with my fists like pistons. I threw ten or twelve punches, my knuckles slick with blood, before I realized he wasn't fighting back.

With his arms spread and my mom screaming at me to stop, he just lay there, his eyes open and locked on mine. His lips were mush, his nose crooked and broken, with one eye already swelling, and I didn't give a shit if he didn't fight back. I'd kill him.

Suddenly a lamp slammed the side of my head and I found myself sprawled on the floor in a daze. Mom, her chest heaving, stood naked over me, still holding the lamp, with tears streaming down her cheeks.

She screamed at me and the words were like fire. "GET OUT!" she said. "GODDAMN YOU TO HELL! GET OUT OF MY HOME!"

I got up from the floor, ignoring her. Conor sat up on the bed, his legs over the edge. He wiped his mouth with the back of his hand as he looked at me. Then he said, "Are you done?"

"Fuck you. Get out," I said.

He shook his head. "That's not up to you."

I lunged for him again and my mom threw the lamp, hitting me square in the chest. Then she lurched for the phone on the nightstand.

"I'm calling the police, Aiden," she said. "So STOP right now!"

"LIARS!" I screamed. "You drunk whore! You're still married!" I said and crossed my arms. "Go ahead, call the police. I'll be out in a day, and the first thing I'll do is off your dirty coward of a boyfriend!"

Conor stood. "I'm here, Aiden. Off me right now."

I reached to my waistband, taking out the pistol Liam had given me. I raised it, pointing it at his chest. He didn't even flinch.

"You don't think I will?" I said.

He nodded. "I think you might."

My mom, her eyes wide, the phone still in her hand, backed up to the window. "Aiden, put the gun down."

"YOU'RE MARRIED!" I screamed.

Her face twisted in rage. "TO A DRUNK WHO BEATS ME! TO A MAN WHO BEATS YOU! I CAN'T EVEN KEEP A JOB BECAUSE OF HIM!"

I swung the barrel toward her, my head pounding. Nothing she said registered. None of it mattered.

"Everything is a lie, Mom, and you're the biggest one, you traitor."

Conor interrupted. "You're mother didn't lie. I asked her not to tell you because I figured you'd think I used you to get to her."

"You did!"

"No. I didn't. I believe in you. I always have."

"Bullshit."

He clenched his jaw. "I'm going to take that thing away from you if you don't point it away from your mother."

Rage exploded through me. "You think you're going to take it from me?" I pointed it at him, cocking the hammer. "Go ahead. Try."

He relaxed. "Thank you. That's much better."

The gun felt heavy and secure in my hand, and he swallowed.

"I know you're upset, Aiden," he said. "I would be, too, and I know how this looks. I know we should have told you from the beginning, but it wasn't the right time."

"You're a liar."

"Maybe I am. But it doesn't change the fact that, no matter how you see things, it's none of your business. Your mother has to decide who she wants to see, not you."

I smirked. "Yeah, just like she wants to send me away so she can screw you any time."

I looked around the room. "You like this, Conor? You want to get your rocks off on a washed-up loser like her for awhile, then dump her? Or do you pay her?"

He shrugged. "See it the way you want, Aiden. You're a man. You've got the gun. But if you don't leave right now, you're going to have to shoot me."

I sneered. "You know what that feels like, huh? Did you tell her you murdered a guy? That you spent ten years in prison?" I looked at my mom. "Great guy, huh? Took blood money for it, too."

Mom nodded, glancing at Conor. "Yes, I know about it. And I know why, too."

"You make me sick. Both of you."

Conor's voice lowered. "Leave, Aiden. Now. We can talk about this when you cool off."

I looked at him and realized the only thing worse than an enemy was somebody who pretended to be a friend.

"The only thing I'm going to do is make your life hell, you prick," I said. "I'm going to own Southie one day, and you know what? You're mine. I'll ruin you."

He nodded. "Put the gun away."

I stared at him, every fiber in me begging to pull the trigger.

"I hate you. Both of you," I said. Then I left.

chapter 39

The next day, Liam sent me to a guy named Mel Cameo, who owned a small, fully furnished rental house on Broadway. He gave it to me for a thousand dollars deposit and a month-to-month lease. The only thing I had to do was pay the utilities, plus eight hundred a month rent, and it was mine for as long as I liked.

I'd missed two driving school classes. But when I showed up and spoke to the teacher, she let me in, handed me the worksheets, and told me to stay late, so I did. It was a breeze. Any nitwit could get a driver's license, and I cracked up laughing, finally understanding why there were so many shitty drivers out there.

I went shopping after class, lugging home plates, cups, utensils, a set of sheets and anything else I could think of that I'd need. Then I went running, stopping off at the pawn shop to say hello to Angel. Her father stood behind the counter when I arrived.

I smiled. "Hello."

He nodded, looking pallid and frail. His hair had

thinned more in the short time since I'd seen him last, and he didn't smile back.

"You kept my daughter out."

"Yessir."

He looked up at me and his eyes changed. They showed resignation, sadness, the battle lost, and I didn't know what else, but it made me feel uneasy. He studied my face, then said, "You shouldn't have."

"I know. And I apologize."

He furrowed his brow. "Sometimes we must learn to live with what we do not like."

"Sometimes."

"You are less than her. *Basura calle*." He spat. "Street trash."

I held his stare and something in me, something that I'd never felt before, kept me calm.

"You can't change this, sir," I told him.

Intense, he studied my face. "I did not work so hard only to die with my daughter disgracing my blood."

"I love her."

"You know nothing of love."

"I know that no matter how much you hate me, I'm going to be with her. And I know there's nothing I can do to change the mind of a racist like you."

"This is the way you speak to a dying man?"

"It's the way I speak to a bitter, selfish bastard who'd rather die with his daughter alone and afraid."

"She does not need you. She is strong. She will go to school. You will stay here and rot in this place."

I took a breath. "Maybe so, but I'll take care of her as long as she's with me."

"Leave. I will speak no more to you."

I walked to the door, then turned, calling to him at the counter. "I'm not trash, sir. I'm good. Your daughter knows that, even if you don't."

Then I turned and left.

chapter 40

"One last string needs to be tied up before we're ready," Liam said.

I nodded.

Tommy stood at his usual place, leaning against the counter and smoking a cigarette.

Liam kept his eyes on me and went on. "His name is Gary Shilling, and you'll be meeting him to pick up payment on a debt."

"How much?"

"Hundred and thirty thousand. We need the capital for the Cuban deal, so I'm collecting early from him."

"When?"

"Tonight."

I nodded.

Liam continued. "I'll have you take Tommy for moral support. I put this guy in a bind, scratching up that kind of cash so soon, and I want to make sure he behaves."

"What's he do?"

Liam smiled. "Runs a high-class escort service, dabbles in coke for his customers, too. Got himself into a bit of a problem with a sting and I smoothed things out for him through a judge I know."

Tommy grunted. "Guy's a prick."

Liam glanced at Tommy. "You're there only for problems, Tommy. Aiden handles the talking."

Tommy's eyes shot bullets at me and he shook his head. Then he said, "Have Lilly and me take care of it. We can handle it just like last time."

"Lilly's on other business," Liam told him.

"But—"

"But, nothing," Liam said, cutting him short. "This isn't a strong-arm deal. He's a good customer, and I make great money from him. Be here at one-fifteen."

chapter **41**

"Don't speed."

Tommy lit another smoke, steering with his knee as he did. We'd borrowed Lilly's cousin's old beater to drive north and Tommy grimaced, exhaling. "You ain't my mother, Aiden."

"You don't have a driver's license."

"Yeah, so?"

"So it'll screw things up if you get pulled over and we get hauled in."

He slowed, talking to the windshield. "King Shit of Turd Mountain speaks."

"What's your problem?" I said.

"I've got no problem, other than you kissing Liam's ass all the time."

I took a breath. This had been coming on for awhile, the tension and looks. I guessed that he was ticked off about Liam giving me the better jobs, that he trusted me and put me in charge, and I knew it.

So I told him, "If you've got something to say, say it."

"Your lips are brown, man."

I clenched my jaw. "How's your mom, huh? You still buying her dope?"

"Shut the fuck up, Aiden."

"Or what? You'll do me like you and Lilly did Ben Capo? You remember him, right?" I mocked. "The guy we shook down that ended up dead?"

He didn't answer.

I studied my friend's profile in the dim. "You lied to me that day."

He kept driving, mute.

"You liked it, didn't you? You liked killing him."

His face cracked into an ugly sneer. "So what if I did? He screwed with Lieam too many times."

That was the answer I didn't want to hear. The answer that showed that this Tommy McAllister wasn't the same Tommy I grew up with. The kid who used to play pranks and had a whip for a mouth, the one who loved his little sister more than life itself, had turned into something sickening. Someone I didn't want to know.

"You're fucked up, Tommy. You know that, don't you? We were tight, man. We were like brothers."

He stared straight ahead. "You should stop talking right now, Aiden. I swear to God on all the years we've been friends, let it go before things get worse."

"No. You lied, man. Remember that time behind the grocery store? We sliced our hands and shook on our blood. We took a vow that said no lies. No cheating. We swore we'd stick together, no matter what."

His mouth was a slit. "We were eight. Things change."

"You've changed, Tommy, not me."

He shook his head, slowing down and shaking another smoke from his pack. "Yeah, I have. And I'm not sorry about it, either." He lit up, then flung the lighter against the windshield. It bounced, sliding across the dash. "I've been shit on all my life, man, and guess what? No matter how, who or what, I will NEVER be that person again. You understand that?"

"You didn't even feel bad about it, did you?"

"About what? Capo? Why should I?"

"Because he didn't deserve it."

He laughed. "Either you get it or you give it, Aiden. What the fuck do you think our lives have been about? How many times did people look at us and see nothing but a couple of poor scumbag kids not worth a shit? We've been getting it since day one in this world, and now it's time to take it back."

"I'm not taking anything back."

"Now who's lying? We're sitting in this car right now for the exact same reasons, man. You like the power and the money, and all the other stuff that goes along with it, so you might as well stop with the bullshit."

"No, I don't like it."

He slammed on the brakes, pulling over. "Then prove it. Get out of the car and walk away."

I sat there, staring out the window at the oncoming headlights, thinking about Angel. "I can't."

"Why? Because you're Liam's bitch now?"

"I do jobs, just like you."

He laughed. "Then you must give one hell of a

blowjob, because something's getting you in good with the boss. Even Lilly hates your guts."

"I told you, I don't like it."

"Then get out of the car. Prove it, big man."

I shook my head. This was going nowhere. "Just drive."

He stuck it in gear, popped the clutch and snorted. "You make the same dirty money I do, Aiden, and not a single dime of it is legit. You're no better than me, pal."

"Maybe not. But I don't like hurting people, Tommy, and you do," I said, wishing that he'd break away and be the old Tommy. The Tommy I knew.

"Maybe you should shut your mouth, huh? I'm tired of your sermons," he said.

I sighed. "Just drive the car, Tommy. And don't start trouble with this guy, either."

"The first time you tell me what to do is the last time."

I stared out the window, letting it go. We drove for awhile, the lines of the highway speeding by, the city turning to suburbs, then dark stretches of nothing but an occasional gas station or motel.

I thought about Mom and Conor, about boxing, Angel's father, school, and my dad, and that's when I realized I'd lost just about everything that mattered. I'd been betrayed by nearly everybody, including Tommy. The best thing to do was to cut the strings, unload all the baggage that was keeping me down.

Like Tommy, I'd promised myself I'd never live the way I had before—poor and struggling, and I felt exactly the same way Tommy did about that. I understood what he meant.

Only problem was, unlike Tommy, I was miserable. I couldn't cut loose. Nothing was resolved; so much of my life was a mess and I didn't know how to fix any of it. I glanced at Tommy and something in me ached. I missed how things used to be between us, how we used to be friends.

I sighed again and asked, "You've met this guy?"

He nodded. "Asshole of the year. Lilly and I picked up his first payment, which he moaned about the whole time." He sneered. "He called me a twelve-year-old. Laughed in my face when I talked."

I swallowed. "This Cuba deal is big."

"Yeah. Good money." A long moment passed, then Tommy flicked his cigarette out the window.

"How is your mom doing?"

"High. How's yours? Still getting porked by that Conor loser?" Tommy said, sarcasm heavy in his voice.

I clenched my teeth, then forced myself to relax. "I was serious."

"So was I."

I looked down at the faint scar on my palm, already years old. The grocery store. Blood brothers. *Things changed*, he'd said. Yeah, they sure did.

I closed my eyes, leaning my head back and realizing I'd lost a friend for good.

Tommy drove on.

chapter 42

Gary Shilling answered the motel room door, looked at both of us, smirked and shook his head. "He sends me the goddamned Boy Scouts. How's that for respect?" Then turned and walked into the room.

We followed and he sat in a chair by a small desk, slumping his stumpy, fat body into it like a slug. He wore a rumpled dress shirt, slacks and a couple of gold rings that matched the gold Star of David on a chain around his neck.

Balding and pale, he ran his hand over his round face. "He has no idea what I did to make this happen," he said, looking toward the bed.

I turned to see what he gazed at.

On the bed was a blonde, her hair mussed and the strap of a nightgown falling off her shoulder, her full breasts barely covered by the sheer material. She gazed at me with drug-clouded eyes.

She giggled and said, "Boys. How cute."

Tommy's eyes lit up in anger.

I cut in before Tommy had the chance to say anything. "Mr. Shilling, do you have the money?"

He nodded, reaching under his chair for a briefcase and sliding it forward. He kicked it toward me. "All of it's here. Payment in full."

I kept my eyes on him, telling Tommy to count it.

Tommy picked up the briefcase and set it on the table, then opened it and started counting.

Shilling glanced at his watch, then at Tommy. "I don't screw people who do me favors," he announced. Then he looked at me. "Tell your boss I appreciated the help. He ever needs anything, he just has to let me know."

Tommy finished counting, nodded, shut the briefcase and handed it to me. It was heavy. "I will," I said and held out my free hand. Shilling took it and we shook.

Tommy, his eyes riveted on the man, held out his hand. As Shilling went to shake it, Tommy grabbed the collar of his shirt and smashed him in the face three times, leaning close to the shocked man.

"You ever disrespect me again, I'll kill you," he said, his voice low and menacing.

Shilling blinked, his eye already swelling and his lip split. "Get out," he said.

Tommy didn't let go, and I sighed. *He's a good customer*, Liam had said. I shook my head. A good customer meant one thing to Liam—money. And Tommy was risking something that wasn't his to risk. "Enough, Tommy. Let's go."

Tommy straightened up, then his eyes roved to the woman. "I'm not done here yet."

Through clenched teeth, I said, "We're leaving. Now."

Tommy walked to the edge of the bed. "You ever see what a *boy* can do, lady?"

She shook her head, her lip quivering.

I grabbed Tommy's shoulder and he flung it off, still facing the girl. "Get out, Aiden. I'm not finished," he said.

"This isn't your deal, Tommy."

He looked at Shilling. "You don't mind if I have a little fun with your girl, right?"

Shilling's face was full of fear and his eyes searched mine. "You don't want to let this happen, kid."

I swallowed. "It won't."

I looked at Tommy. "This isn't me talking, Tommy. You do this and Liam will make you pay. You know it, too."

Tommy pulled his pistol, jacked the action back and pointed it at my head. "I told you the first time you tell me what to do will be the last. Nobody talks to me that way, and this bitch and her pimp are going to learn that."

His eyes bored into mine. "Now, I said I'm not done. You going to watch, or are you going to leave?"

I looked at Mr. Shilling, who had a pleading look in his eyes, then back to Tommy. Dread filled me. I could tell by the expression on Tommy's face that he'd kill me. That he *wanted* to kill me. This was Tommy's kind of power, and it had no boundaries. And he'd do anything to feel it.

I wasn't about to die for it, either. So I left, sick to my stomach, disgusted with myself for letting it happen and knowing that things *had* changed forever between me and Tommy.

chapter **43**

I didn't tell Liam about what happened at the motel room. Either Shilling would let him know or it would fade away into nothing. But I had to admit that what I'd seen there—especially that look in Tommy's eyes—scared me. And I had a bad feeling that there would be consequences for whatever had happened in that room.

He'd come out of the motel room fifteen minutes after I'd left, got in the car and hadn't said a word the entire way home. There'd been no gunshots, so I figured nobody had been killed, but I blocked any further thought about what he'd done to that woman. It made me want to vomit.

The Cuban deal was on for tonight, and my heart beat slow and steady as I walked up G Street, on my way to meet Angel for a cup of coffee when school let out. "Business was business," Liam always said. And this was big business. A one-shot deal, he'd said, and that you always have to be careful with people in this life. He told me that even though the ones closest to you are the ones that usually screw you over, the ones you don't know could be just as dangerous.

There would be four of us meeting the Cubans tonight, enough to take care of any problems for sure, but still, I was nervous. For once I was glad Lilly would be around. I kicked a rock and laughed to myself, thinking, *If there's a rabid pit bull in the house, better to have him on your side.* I'd heard that somewhere and there was truth to it. In the company of bad people, having the worst on your team was a good thing, especially when the loser could end up dead.

Arriving at our meeting place, I stood outside the school fence and watched the kids stream out of the buildings in a wave of color and noise.

Then I heard someone say, "Mr. O'Connor."

I turned to find Mr. Langdon, my old English teacher, standing there. "Hi," I said.

He nodded, as awkward as usual, with his leather satchel hanging over his shoulder. "How are you?" he asked.

"I still have that book, if you're wondering. I forgot to return it," I told him.

"I didn't loan it to you. It was a gift."

I studied his face. "Thanks."

"My pleasure," he said and looked around. "You know, sometimes I wonder about this place."

"The school?"

"Yes."

"What's to wonder?"

"We're here to help build the future of the students we serve, yet I wonder who we really serve."

I smiled. "Lost me there, Mr. Langdon."

He shrugged. "Oftentimes, Mr. O'Connor, those who

need the most help are cast out for reasons incompatible with our goals. I've been thinking about our conversation at the jewelry store."

"Me, too."

He studied my face for a moment. "Even I've been hearing the whispers, Aiden. You seem to be—" He stopped. "Are you okay?"

"The Golden Rule."

He raised his eyebrows. "Yes? And what about it?"

I shrugged. "You weren't saying *not* to hurt anybody, were you?"

"No, I wasn't. It's inevitable."

"You were saying to choose what will hurt the least, huh?"

He nodded.

"Sometimes that's hard to figure out," I said.

"It is. But we have a helper."

"A helper?"

He tapped his head, smiling. "Sometimes the first thing we ignore when confronted with a conflict is our conscience. Unfortunately, a conscience holds little weight against other things."

"Like what?"

"Greed, selfishness, anger, bitterness and need."

"Need?"

He nodded. "You feel you need things, Aiden." He eyed me. "I won't pretend to ignore your ties to certain people in this city. I also won't hesitate to tell you that sometimes the end result, however good, does not justify the path traveled to get it."

"What are you saying?"

"I'm saying that this place," he pointed at the school, "has the potential to bring you as much success as your other choices. It's just a different, and sometimes longer, path."

I swallowed. "It's hard, you know? I...just don't see how it would work." I grunted. "They won't even let me on campus."

He smiled. "The righteous path is always harder. But a clear conscience lets us sleep at night so we're able to get up and work harder to achieve it."

I furrowed my brow, but before I could ask him what the hell he was talking about, Angel came around the corner and smiled. "Hi," she said and pecked me on the cheek, then turned to the teacher. "Hello, Mr. Langdon."

He nodded to her and said, "Hello." Then he began shuffling away from us, saying, "Well, I'm off. It was nice seeing you, Aiden."

"Yeah, thanks."

Then he was gone. Angel took a stick of gum from her purse and asked what our conversation had been about.

I shrugged. "I don't know. He's strange."

She smiled. "He's the coolest teacher at this school."

I took her backpack and we began walking.

She looked at her feet. "I took my dad to the emergency room last night."

"Oh, yeah?"

She nodded.

"He had a seizure. The doctor said it was because the brain tumor was causing pressure as it grows."

"Want to go visit him?"

She shook her head. "He refused to be admitted. The doctor had a fit when he made me take him home."

"I don't blame him," I said.

"Who? The doctor?"

"No, your dad. I wouldn't stay there, either."

She bit her lip. "His system is shutting down. They told me he'd be gone in anywhere from a few days to a week. I wanted to stay home with him today, but he insisted I go to school."

I thought about his words to me. "He loves you."

She smiled. "He's just so stubborn, and things have been horrible between us lately." She looked away. "I heard him talk to you the other day. I'm sorry, but I didn't know what to do."

I stopped walking and turned to face her. "He wants the best for you, and he's doing what he thinks is right. It's not his fault."

Tears glistened in her eyes. "I just wish—"

I shook my head. "It doesn't matter, Angel. Really."

"It matters to me."

I smiled. "I know, but this is about him, not us. He's just worried about you."

She sniffed. "Things are going to be bad, Aiden."

"How?"

"I've looked through his files. He has a twenty-thousand-dollar life insurance policy, but I also found out he also has over thirty thousand in debt. And that's why nobody will buy the shop—because of all that debt the business owes."

223

"Will you have to pay it?"

"I don't think so, but the insurance money will be gone. I tried to talk to him about it, but he didn't want to."

"You can live with me."

"I promised him when I was fourteen that I wouldn't live with a man unless I was married."

"Then marry me."

She sighed. "Now who's being crazy? I'm not getting married just so I can live somewhere. Besides, we're too young and I'm not ready."

"Then I'll get you a place. And if it makes you feel better, you can pay me back later. When you finish college."

"I'll just get a job."

I realized then that Angel and her father were the same in a lot of ways and I smiled. "Do you trust me?" I asked her.

She rolled her eyes. "Of course. Don't be stupid."

"Then how about you rent the room upstairs at my place? All on the up and up. Purely a business deal. You get a part-time job, pay me a hundred bucks a month, and we're good."

She stared off down the street for a minute. "Maybe."

I shrugged. "Think about it. No strings attached. I promise."

"We'll see."

I nodded. "Sure. Now I suppose you came out to tell me that coffee is off and that you should go home to see after your father."

She smiled. "Yes. I'm sorry."

I kissed her. "I'll see you tomorrow, then."

The security guard sleeping in the booth at the gate of the Longshoreman's Dock woke up when he heard the car. He recognized Liam sitting in the passenger seat, nodded and let us pass.

Liam grinned. "He's my cousin."

Lilly parked the car as the thunder of a jetliner about to land at Logan Airport passed overhead. We sat in the darkness.

Tommy lit a cigarette next to me in the back seat, his voice tinged with excitement. "How many of them will there be?"

Liam's reply was low and quiet. "One, maybe two. We'll just keep our eyes open. Lilly, you'll hang back and to the left, Tommy on the right, and Aiden, you'll carry the money."

"What's the street value?" Tommy asked.

"Over two million."

I looked at the duffel bag at my feet. "How much is in the bag?"

"Five hundred thousand."

"Holy shit," I said.

"Holy shit is right," Liam said. "This deal HAS to go down without a hitch. Any problems, shoot first and talk later. Got it?"

Tommy cackled and Lilly grunted. I looked out the window, peering into the fog rolling in from the water. Mr. Langdon flitted through my mind as I said, "Sure."

"Everybody packing?" Liam said.

Lilly grunted again. Tommy slid his pistol out, checked it, then said, "Yep."

I shifted, feeling the bulge of the revolver in my waistband. My heart skipped a beat as I said, "Yes."

Liam opened the door. "Let's go."

A huge ship loomed to our left, docked and full of imported cars from Japan, and as we made our way to the meeting place, the sounds of the ocean—creaking timbers, lapping water and the occasional splash—made the hair on my arms stand on end. The fog got thicker the farther out we walked and soon the buildings became shadows against the white fog, materializing as we came closer.

Then Liam stopped. I stepped close to him. "We need to talk, Liam," I said, Mr. Langdon's words swirling in my mind.

Liam studied the pier. "Not now."

"I know. After this, though," I said.

He nodded. Lilly moved off to the side and back a few steps, scanning the area, and Tommy stuck his hand in the coat pocket where his pistol lay.

I clutched the bag of cash and asked, "Now what?"

"We wait," Liam said.

So we did, and in the hushed quiet, the tension was almost as thick as the fog around us. My scalp prickled and I shivered. I was holding half a million dollars. People I knew from the projects wouldn't make that much in thirty years.

Then, in the distance, I caught movement out of the corner of my eye, just a shadow of something that wasn't there a second before.

Liam tensed and said, "There's a requirement for this deal," he whispered, keeping his eyes on the shape slowly appearing before us.

I took a deep breath. "What requirement?"

He went on. "I've got to know you're loyal, Aiden."

The way he said it, low and steady, made my stomach shrink. "What is it, Liam?"

"In order to stop the war we had going with the Roxbury people, part of the compromise I made was that this guy would be gone. They see him as a threat to their business, even if he is a lone player, and I agreed because I didn't have many cards left to play with them." He gestured to the money bag. "Two hundred thousand of that cash will go to them as peace money, and in return I get a price cut on supplies. We also keep the merchandise from this deal."

The shape came closer. He was dragging something, and as his silhouette became clear through the fog, I guessed it was a suitcase on rollers with two million dollars worth of dope inside. Fear gripped me. "You said something about my loyalty…"

"*You'll* be getting rid of this guy tonight. You're in too far now. You've got to prove yourself." He said with a finality that sent a shiver down my spine.

My breath caught. My lungs froze. The man approached, cautious and slow. Panic tore through me. "Liam, I don't think I can…" I stuttered.

He looked at me. "It's your last step, Aiden. There's no turning back."

I almost crumpled. There it was, out in the open. Conor's insistance that I'd have to eventually kill somebody crashed through me. I knew right then that no matter how Liam felt about me, business was business, and nothing would stop him. If I refused to kill this guy, I'd be dead instead.

Liam spoke to me just before the figure was close enough to hear. "We make sure he has the goods, then you do your job."

I had nothing to say. I was a fool for thinking I could play this game and not pay for it, and now, the consequences were in plain sight. In a flash, I knew what happened with Conor. He'd been me, and he'd made a choice. Kill or be killed.

The dealer I'd been ordered to kill came closer, and as he reached us, I stared at him. My heart nearly stopped.

Angel's father stood before us.

◆

Recognition lit his eyes, and in an instant, as our eyes met, a world of understanding opened up before us. I knew why he was doing this. I didn't care how or why he knew the people in Cuba to get the dope, but I knew enough to realize his past was my future, and he'd recognized it in me. He knew what street trash was because he'd been street trash. I also knew this deal wasn't for him. He was doing it for Angel. He'd come to America to get away from this, but he'd do anything for his daughter.

Lilly laughed. "Well, don't you know, fellas. It's the old man from the pawn shop."

Tommy looked at me, and judging by the gleam in his eyes and the wicked smile on his face, he knew who the man was. And he was enjoying it.

Liam nodded to Mr. Vives and said, "Open the case."

But Angel's father, his voice weak, said, "I need to see the money first." He kept his eyes down, almost in shame.

Liam gestured to the bag. "Open it."

I was in an alternate reality; this wasn't really happening. I opened the bag, showing him the money.

Mr. Vives swallowed, then slowly bent, opening the case, exposing the packages. Liam nodded to Tommy, who stepped forward and took one. He slit it open with a pocket knife, dipped a finger into the powder and tasted it. "It's real," he said.

I was paralyzed. Liam nodded once more, and Lilly and Tommy drew their weapons. Liam, his face straight, spoke. "There's been a change of plans."

Mr. Vives raised his head, eyes lit with alarm, and as he glanced over to me, the fire in them died. His shoulders slumped and he bowed his head again, speaking softly in Spanish. He took a deep breath, his frail chest shuddering, then he looked at me. "You know this was for her, and now you will take it."

Liam looked at me, then drew his pistol. "You'd better talk fast, Aiden. What's this about?"

I forced the words out. "He's my girl's father, and he's dying from brain cancer. He's doing this for her so she'll have something when he's gone. She has nothing, otherwise."

Liam took a deep breath, his words sharp and cutting. "This is *business*, goddammit! And you know it has to happen!"

I looked at Liam. "I know it does."

He clenched his teeth. "Then do it, Aiden."

I hesitated.

"DO IT!" he growled.

Tommy cut in. "He doesn't have the stones, boss." He looked at me. "He never has. He's just a pussy that thinks he's better than everybody else, but he ain't got the spine."

Liam glared at Tommy. "Shut up."

Tommy laughed. "What a joke," he said, raising his pistol to Mr. Vives. "Give me the word and I'll plug him. Straight through his sick head."

Liam grunted, then looked at Tommy. "Do you realize how much money you cost me with Shilling and your little tantrum? Eighty grand a year, Tommy, and all because you're stupid. Just like you're being stupid now." With that, Liam swung his pistol up and pointed it at Tommy's forehead. "You really think you're worth eighty grand a year?" he asked.

Tommy held his breath, fear in his eyes. He said nothing in the still night air.

Liam pulled the trigger.

Tommy's body stiffened as he fell to the dock, his body thudding against the planks. Mr. Vives stood still, no expression on his face.

Liam lowered his weapon and looked at me. "Tommy didn't have a choice tonight, Aiden. You do. Make your choice—now."

I looked at Mr. Vives. "I'm sorry about this, sir. I'm sorry about everything," I said, then reached into my pocket, taking my pistol out. I turned to Liam. "I gave my word to Mr. Vives that I'd take care of his daughter. Killing her father and stealing the money isn't taking care of her," I said, then held the pistol out for him to take. "I'm not doing it, Liam."

Lilly reached out and grabbed the pistol from my hand. Liam raised his pistol to my head. "You're willing to die for it, then."

I nodded. "Tommy was right. It's not in me. I can't kill. I can't live with this anymore."

I expected a bullet to rip through my brain, but Liam didn't pull the trigger. He just laughed, shaking his head in wonder. "You really do love her, don't you?"

I swallowed. "Yes, I do, but it's more than that. I just can't do this."

His face hardened. "Lilly, go back to the car," he said.

Lilly blinked, confused. "You sure, boss?"

"Yes. The old man won't do anything. Go."

Lilly disappeared into the fog.

Liam nudged the barrel against my forehead, his eyes looking directly into mine. "Did you know that you were supposed to be my son?"

My mind reeled, and I had the feeling that the last pieces of the puzzle were finally fitting together. "No," I said.

He gripped the pistol tighter, and his words rushed out. "I've kept track of you since the day you were born. I've arranged for every job your mother ever got, every raise she received, and I tried to help Nick when he lost his job and started drinking. I tried."

I gaped. "Why?"

His jaw muscles tensed. "I loved your mother, Aiden. I loved her with everything I had. I still do. I would have died for her, just like right now you'd die for your girl. But she chose Nick, and there was nothing I could do about that."

"I—I don't know what to say."

Liam's eyes grew distant, like he was in another place. "The first time your father hit her, before you were born, she came to me. She was scared and unsure," he said, blinking, his eyes focusing on mine again. "We made love that night."

My breath caught. "What are you saying?"

He shook his head. "I don't know if that night made you, Aiden, and it doesn't really matter. She chose Nick, and it's probably for the better, because I'm not a good person. But I can't kill what could be my son," he said, lowering the pistol. Then he nudged the bag of money with his toe. "I wanted you to rule Southie, but I was wrong about it. You can't be me, and you're willing to die for it," he said. Then he looked at Mr. Vives. "Take the money, old man. Go home."

Mr. Vives nodded, shuffling forward. He looked at me for a moment, then spoke. "Take care of my daughter."

Minutes passed as the old man waddled from the dock, dragging the bag of money behind him. I looked at the suitcase with the drugs in it. "What now?"

Liam looked at me. "Never speak to anybody about what I told you."

I nodded. "What about the two hundred grand you'll owe the Roxbury people? I'll pay it back somehow."

He studied my face. "Tommy wasn't worth eighty grand, Aiden. Let's just say you're worth two hundred." He smiled. "Besides, the dope in that case is worth two million. I'll be fine."

I took a breath. "I don't know what to say."

"Go box, Aiden, and forget you ever knew me."

Epilogue

Angel's father died six days later. He passed away in his own bed, just the way he wanted it, his last breath witnessed by his daughter sitting next to him, holding his hand.

I visited him the day before his death, expecting nothing and everything at the same time. And as I sat in the wooden chair beside his bed, he hadn't said a word. He just looked at me. When it was time to go, I said goodbye and he nodded. That was all.

We both knew the unspoken would be forever unspoken. Whether it was honor among thieves or honor among men who were willing to forsake what was right to do good, I didn't know. But in his eyes, I could see that his life was not all that different from mine. Angel would never know about that night on the dock. We all make choices, and sometimes those choices hurt. He came to America all those years ago to get away from the very thing he ended up needing to help his daughter.

The day after Mr. Vives died, a gentleman from New York City visited Angel. He wore a Rolex watch and a thousand-dollar suit, and in his briefcase he carried an investment portfolio in her name worth four hundred thousand dollars. I have no idea how her father had washed the cash so quickly, but he had somehow, and I didn't care.

The only thing I knew was that Mr. Vives had died making choices that hurt everybody, and he'd chosen who to hurt the least.

Angel closed down the pawn shop over the next few months, and true to her father's wishes, she refused to move in with me, instead renting a place just a few blocks from mine. She bought a dog, kept up her grades, and graduated high school with honors.

I love her, and she loves me back. I asked her to marry me and she laughed at my persistence. Yes, she'd said. But not now. Until then, she's wearing the promise ring on her wedding finger.

As for me, well, with the help of Mr. Langdon, I was reinstated and went back to school. I'd screwed off so much since I was a freshman that by the end of the year, I didn't have enough credits to graduate. But I stuck it out anyway, then went to summer school and my diploma eventually came in the mail.

I got my driver's license, took a job working down at the docks offloading cars coming from Japan, and I'm training at a gym across town. I'd had three fights since Mr. Vives died and I won all of them.

I'm thinking of becoming a cop, of all things. Ironically, I'd probably see my father more often that way.

It took me two months to build up the nerve to talk to my mom. When I heard that she'd moved in with Conor, I stewed for days until I realized that it really wasn't any of my business.

I knew what the right thing to do was, but knowing it and doing are two very different things and sometimes it's a killer. The first time I showed up at Conor's place, the three of us sat in his living room and it ended with a shouting match. I slammed his front door so hard when I left, I broke the window in it.

A week later, Conor came to my house and we talked.

I didn't feel the urge to pound his head into the pavement that time, and I don't know whether I began believing he didn't use me to get to my mother or if I just figured out that it didn't matter. The main thing is he loves my mother. She also filed for a divorce a few weeks ago.

We met last week for dinner and things were okay. Conor opened up the door to my coming back to the gym, telling me that whenever I was ready, I was welcome. And he congratulated me on winning my matches. I've been thinking about going back to him ever since and might give it a try.

Angel doesn't understand why the situation between my mom and Conor creates so much anger in me; honestly, I don't really know, either. I guess I just wish my parents had been able to have a regular marriage, and because they didn't, I'm holding it against Conor. I know it's not right, but I can't help it. It's just the way it is.

I didn't go to Tommy's funeral. I couldn't bring myself to face his family, and I couldn't really face what had happened. He was dead. I'd seen him killed by a man that might be my father, and for now at least, it's something I don't like thinking about. Tommy being gone hurt his family, I knew, but I didn't know if him being here would have ended up hurting more. I also try to remember Tommy the way he used to be, not the way he ended up. Sometimes life just plain sucks.

So now, as I'm lacing up my shoes and getting ready to take a run, I think about that day at the jewelry store. I think about the Golden Rule, and that honor equals honesty.

I learned a lot from Liam, too, and even though he ignores me if we see each other on the street, he reminds me that we all have to make choices. Even if they hurt.

Acknowledgments

Special thanks to George Nicholson, my agent at Sterling Lord Literistic Inc., for always believing in me, and to Erica Silverman for all her help and valuable input.

Thank you to Evelyn Fazio, my fantastic editor, for believing wholeheartedly in this story.

Thanks to my friends and family for their constant encouragement and to Michelle for her guidance and unyielding support.

Thanks to Michael Harmon for all his hard work in perfecting this story and for the opportunity to work with a brilliant author.

While growing up in Southie certainly had its challenges, they have provided me with a wealth of experiences that have inspired me in my writing, for which I am grateful.

—John Shea

Special thanks go to my agent, George Nicholson, of Sterling Lord Literistic, Inc, and his fantastic and spot-on assistant, Erica Silverman.

Evelyn Fazio, my editor, thank you.

To John Shea: thanks, man. This has been quite a ride, eh?

—Michael Harmon